I Believe in Water

twelve brushes with religion

I Believe in Water

edited by marilyn singer

HARPERCOLLINS*PUBLISHERS*

To those who doubt, and those who don't

The poem "To a Jewish Friend, Wearing Green" by Marie McAuliff
that appears on pages 49–50 was first published in *The Washington Post*
in 1946 and is used with permission.

Library of Congress Cataloging-in-Publication Data
I believe in water : twelve brushes with religion / edited by Marilyn Singer.
   p.   cm.
   Summary: An anthology of stories for teenagers, exploring the topics of religion,
belief, and spirituality by award-winning authors, including M. E. Kerr, Kyoko Mori,
and Virginia Euwer Wolff.
   ISBN 0-06-028397-1 — ISBN 0-06-028398-X (lib. bdg.)
   1. Religions—Juvenile Fiction.   2. Spirituality—Juvenile fiction.   3. Children's
stories, American. [1. Religions—Fiction.   2. Spirituality—Fiction.   3. Short
Stories.] I. Singer, Marilyn.
PZ5. I18   2000   00-26773
[Fic]—dc21   CIP
                                                   AC

Typography by Alison Donalty
1 3 5 7 9 10 8 6 4 2
❖   First Edition

Acknowledgments

Many thanks to: Bill and Michele Aronson; Bob and Laura Aronson; Debbie and Jerry Aronson; Dena Aronson; Steve Aronson; Michele Coppola; Simone Kaplan; Jay Kerig; Donn, Susan, Sara and Amy Livingston; David Lubar; Joe Morton; Ernest and Rebecca Porcelli; Dian Curtis Regan; Susan Tuchman; Julia Watts; Asher Williams; Van Wolverton; and especially to Matt Rosen, who helped start this project; to Renée Cafiero, Anne Hoppe, Robin Stamm, Robert Warren and the rest of the Harper crew; and to the amazing writers featured in this book.

Contents

Nancy Springer

THE BOY WHO CALLED GOD SHE

So there's this new kid in school, see? One of my suckups, little freshman punk, saw him go in the office and let me know. So me'n Brent take a stroll to peep him out, because the two of us basically run the school, I mean the important stuff, like who gets to yank lunch money and jump line and go in the bathroom whenever they want.

"Loser," Brent says to me out of the side of his mouth.

"Geek," I agree, because the new kid is skinny and dorky-looking with a softie face and purple fruity-ass hair, thinks he's hot snot but he's not. If he was, he wouldn't be all about the dress code. This is a Christian school, and boys are supposed to wear dark slacks and a button-front shirt and a tie. My parents send me here because they say it will teach me a sense of order and discipline. Yeah, right. My parents don't go to church or anything, but they think Jesus is good for kids, kind of like Santa Claus. Like, they sent me to Sunday school when I was little. What I mostly learned was that I gotta be good or I go to Hell. So I figure I'm gonna go to Hell, because I am definitely not good and I like to beat up on geeks, and it looks like God just sent me another one.

Just as I'm thinking this, buttface Mrs. Miller clops up in those horseshoes of hers. "Put your tie on, Derek," she snarfs at me.

"It is on." Tied around my head.

"Put it on properly."

Stupid old hippie, doesn't she know a proper headband when she sees one? "But Mrs. Miller, it's keeping my hair orderly and disciplined."

She isn't buying it. No damn sense of humor. I take the tie off my head and duck in the bathroom like I need a mirror or something and stick the tie in my back pocket. Then me'n Brent have a smoke. Then we hang out. By third period we get bored and go to class. I pull my shirttails half out of my pants to give the teachers something else to bother me about.

Third period is Religion class—like all the classes ain't religion? I mean, in this school we got Jesus algebra, for Christ's sake. But anyway, the new kid, I mean candy-ass, is there. It turns out his name is Julian, which doesn't make me like him any better. I dump my butt in a seat in the back of the room and stare at Julian's skinny neck and his grape-jelly hair without thinking much about him or listening much to anything until up goes his hand and he says it.

"I don't think God means for us to be scared of Her," he says.

Her??

That bumps me up straight. I'm staring at this weird kid. Everybody is staring. Including the teacher. He can't seem to think what to say. There is this awesomely total silence, like a white hole of no noise at all.

Finally the teacher—Reverend Weltzer; he's a preacher at some church on Sundays—finally he says like each word is an egg that might break and make a slimy mess, "You refer to God as 'Her,' Julian?"

And that geek Julian says "Yes" with kind of a question mark on it, like, isn't that okay?

Weltzer says, "May I ask why?"

"I, uh, I just do." The fruithead doesn't sound real sure of himself.

"But our Lord Jesus was male," Weltzer says. "And he referred to God as his Father."

"Because it made God easy for him to talk to!" Julian lights up, dorky happy.

"I, um, I suppose so . . ." Now Weltzer isn't sure.

Julian says, "See, that's it. For me God's easy to talk to if She's a Her."

Just listening to him I want to crawl under the chair. Embarrassed to be human. I mean, what an unbelievable loser.

Reverend Weltzer thinks so too. I can see it in his face. He goes on talking about obedience or whatever and doesn't call on Julian anymore.

After class I pass Julian in the hall and knock him good with my shoulder. Brent lays in right behind me and goes, "Ew, a bug!" and whacks him hard on his fruit-loop head.

"Hey!" the dork yells at both of us, but we just laugh and keep walking.

At home I have to eat dinner with my parents, and just for something to say besides pass the beans, I tell them, "There's this new kid in my school who calls God 'She.'"

Mom and Dad both look at me like I just flashed them.

"She," I say it again for them. "Her. God. Like, the big mama in the sky."

"Is this girl some sort of radical feminist, Derek?" my dad wants to know.

"Girl? What girl?"

"It's a *boy* doing this?" Mom goes, all shocked.

"No duh, Mom." Like, how many other genders are there? Don't answer that.

She ignores the sarcasm. "He must be some kind of sissy."

Dad says, "I hope Reverend Weltzer told him to put a cork in it."

I just shrug. I don't want to agree with my mom or my dad even though I kind of do agree.

I don't have to say anything because somebody knocks at the door. It's Brent. I go out on the sidewalk with him and have a smoke. We talk about some stuff, and then he says, "What about that nerd Julian? How can any human being get that stupid?"

Actually, I can't believe anyone *can* be that stupid. "You think maybe he's tugging on Weltzer's chain?" If he was, I wish I'd thought of it first.

"Nah. He's as serious as a heart attack, man."

"So what's his problem?"

"I don't know. Weltzer should tell him to stuff it where the sun don't shine."

The next day me'n Brent see Julian in the lobby before school. He has his hair in a Statue of Liberty with each spike a different color. Brent shoves him up against a pillar, and I grab his bookbag and dump his papers and stuff all over the floor. This time he doesn't even say "Hey." He just looks at us. See, he's not so stupid. He's learning.

He doesn't seem to be learning real fast in Religion,

though. Weltzer starts class with about sixteen reasons from the Bible why God is a He, and up goes Julian's hand. "But that was back *then*," he says.

Weltzer says, all preacherish and really getting into it, "But Jesus is still here for us today! Christ arose from the dead. He—"

"God's alive, right?"

"Yes! Exactly!"

"So when you're alive, you grow, you change? Like it was Yahweh in the Old Testament and in the New Testament it's Jesus and everything's changed?"

Weltzer starts to turn colors. It's interesting. His nose gets white, and the same around the mouth and eyes, but the rest of his face gets pink like those Styrofoam tomatoes they slice for sandwiches in the cafeteria. He says between his teeth, "But then Jesus said his ministry was conclusive. He said, I am the Way—"

"But if God is alive, She can change Her mind anytime She wants, can't She?"

Girls are giggling, Brent is laughing out loud, and me, I'm snickering but I'm listening to every word. I've never paid so much attention in class before.

Weltzer says, edgy like a knife, "Julian, it is not consistent with Christian tradition to refer to our Lord by a female pronoun."

"But what if She's tired of being locked in the Bible?"

"Julian—"

Julian says, real soft, "You don't want to listen. When I talk to Her, She listens."

The whole class bursts out laughing, and I'm watching Julian and I see his neck get red. Weltzer gets red too, pissed off, like we're laughing at him. He barks, "In this school we refer to the deity as He."

That loser Julian just doesn't know when to give up. He says, "But if She's alive . . . I mean, I'm alive, so I change. Like, I changed my hair today. What if She—"

Weltzer tells him, "Julian, report to the office."

"Huh? Why?"

"Your hair is in violation of the dress code. Go."

That's a crock. Weltzer just doesn't want to argue anymore, at least not about God being a guy. He's probably expecting an argument about the hair, but—this is weird—Julian doesn't say a thing. He just gets up and walks out looking like he's been hit, and that's weird too, because he didn't look that way when Brent was threatening his life. Dumb fruit-for-hair. Hell, who cares about getting sent to the office? If it was Brent or me, we would strut out. Three times and you get paddled, so what? They gotta do better than that to make me orderly and disciplined.

•   •   •

I see Julian in the hall before lunch. His hair is wet and slicked down on his head. So I give him a shove. "Hey, rat face, you need a crying towel?"

He just looks at me, and all of a sudden I notice his eyes, sky gray, so calm and deep they're freaky.

Brent comes up and whacks him on the back of the head and starts to say—

I don't know what. Because Julian spins around and shoves Brent so hard, he slams him against the lockers. And before I can blink, he grabs me like no damn problem and slams me alongside of Brent. Knocks the breath out of me. Next thing I know, he has a hand under my chin and slides me up the locker slick as an elevator. Brent too. He lifts both of us right off our feet.

The whole hallway is dead white-hole silent, nobody moving, everybody watching. I can hear my heart pounding and I'm trying to breathe and I can't even think to use my hands, I'm just hoping Julian will let me down soon now please.

He says, very quiet, almost sweet, "Leave—me—alone." Then he lets go. Me'n Brent drop to our feet.

We stand there rubbing the red spots under our jawbones and watching Julian stalk off toward the cafeteria with everybody getting out of his way.

Here comes my freshman punk suckup. "I hear he's a swimmer," he says. "You got to watch them. They're skinny but they're really strong."

"Yeah, I hear he's training for the Olympics," says another ass-kisser.

"I hear he bench presses one-forty."

Brent says, "Shut up." His voice comes out squeaky, but they zip it and back away.

Brent looks at me. I look at Brent. "This calls for revenge," Brent says.

I don't say anything. My voice box feels sorta numb.

At supper, Mom asks me, "Is that new boy still making trouble at your school?"

"Huh?" I get kind of slow when I don't want to talk.

"The sissy boy. The one who says God is a woman."

"Oh." Julian. "He's not a 'sissy boy.'" God, my mother is so out of it.

"He's not?"

"No." A maniac, maybe, a nut case, riding the short bus. Freaky as hell. But definitely not a wimp or a geek either.

So much for sizing up new kids.

The next day Weltzer sends Julian to the office again. Says his tie violates the dress code. It's a hand-painted tie with a picture of a woman in a white gown sitting on a throne in the middle of an oval of golden stars. Weltzer says it's from the Tarot and it's Satanic. I am sitting right there with my shirt hanging out and no tie on and he doesn't send me to the damn office.

Weltzer is a major crock.

I see Julian in the hall around lunchtime, but I let him alone. So does Brent.

Me'n Brent been buddies practically since kindergarten, but that day we don't have a whole lot to say to each other. We walk out slow after school. Neither of us can think of anything fun to do.

Until I see Weltzer's car. There it sits at the far end of the parking lot, a gray Ford Escort with a Jesus fish window sticker and "You've Got a Friend in JESUS Pennsylvania" on the front license plate and some bumper stickers on the back—"Don't Drive Faster Than Your Angel Can Fly," that sort of thing. Me'n Brent walk past it and I say, "Whoa." Weltzer has a bright new bumper sticker:

GOD IS NOT POLITICALLY CORRECT, BUT HE'S RIGHT

Big black letters. The minute I see it—I can't explain what makes the thought fly into my head, but I just have to do it. It's gonna make him so pissed.

"Gimme a black marker, Brent!"

"Huh?"

"A black marker! In your book bag, dork! Give it!"

I'm not worried about somebody seeing me, what with all the cars roaring past between me and school. Anyhow, it takes only a minute. A quick curved line, an S:

GOD IS NOT POLITICALLY
CORRECT, BUT SHE'S RIGHT

"You been around Julian too much" is all Brent says.

I don't say a thing; I just grin. See, I'm bad.

But get this: I'm so big and bad, I never once figure that Julian will get blamed.

First thing next day, about half a minute into homeroom period, Weltzer's voice blares over the intercom, yelling for Julian to report to the office.

Not like me'n Brent are in homeroom. We are hanging out in our private office, by the urinals. But there's a speaker in the bathroom too. We hear it. And at the same time we both get it, what's happening. I look at Brent and he looks at me.

He goes all round-eyed. "Perfect!" he whispers.

I don't say anything.

"Derek, my man . . ." He whacks me on the back. "The perfect revenge."

I don't say anything.

"Paddle central, here comes Julian!"

I don't say anything. I look at Brent, my buddy. Since kindergarten, or first grade anyway. Both of us in this so-called Christian school because our parents hope it will straighten us out.

I head toward the door.

"Hey man, where you going?"

I don't answer. I just go charging out.

I run mach 100 down the empty hallway and skid into the office just in time. Weltzer is yanking Julian toward the back room, the principal is waiting in the doorway, and Julian—I mean, I never met anybody with more guts, the way he stuck up for his She-God, but he doesn't need this. He isn't fighting Weltzer, but Weltzer is giving him the rough hand anyway, and Julian just looks sick.

"It was me!" I yell, barging in.

Weltzer swings around with his head jutting out like he's a ticked-off bear. He gives me the glare, his face like he has hives, he is so pumped full of high blood pressure and preacher wrath. "What do you—" he starts to yell at me.

But I yell at him instead. "It was me put the damn S on your asshole bumper sticker!"

Well, that does it. I mean, how would I know what it was all about if I didn't do it? They have to let Julian go. I am the one who gets to experience the joy of the back room.

But while I'm in there I have a talk with the principal. Me and the principal kind of understand each other in a weird way, he is so used to hitting me. He's seen me bullshit him so much, he knows this time something's different. I tell him what's been happening with Weltzer and Julian, and he listens.

After I'm finished, he thinks about it a couple minutes.

"Vandalism was not the right way to handle it," he says finally.

"I wasn't trying to handle anything!"

"Well . . . you're trying to handle it now, aren't you, Derek?"

Give me a break. "Just paddle me and let me go."

"Paddle a rescuing hero? I don't think so. You try to stay out of trouble now, you hear?"

I can't believe it. But no problem, the principal gives me a pass back to class. I can tell by his face he's still thinking about what I said, and I know he can't say so, but I think he's going to have a little talk with Weltzer. Maybe Julian won't get sent to the office again just for saying what he believes.

Guess what. Julian is supposed to be in class but he's a bad boy out in the hall, waiting for me around the first corner. He reaches out a hand to stop me. "Thanks," he says, his voice almost a whisper.

I growl, "Thanks for what?"

"What you did . . ."

"I didn't do anything but act stupid."

"But I—you—"

I don't want him trying to thank me. Anyway, it's all kind of his fault. I burst out, "Why do you call God She, anyway?"

"Why not?"

"But do you believe it?"

He shrugs.

"You think God's got *boobs*?"

"You think She's got a wanker?"

I can't deal with this. I don't know what to think anymore. I say, almost begging him, "You're just doing it to yank Weltzer's chain, right?"

He shakes his head. "No."

"Then *why*?"

He smiles at me. And his sky-gray eyes are quiet and happy and really freaky under that purple hair, like he's a crazy angel. He smiles, the bell rings, he walks away.

Next day Weltzer sort of apologizes to the whole Religion class for being a turd, except that's not what he calls it, but Julian is not there. Julian is not in school the next day, either, or the next.

I haven't seen him since.

I keep looking for him at malls and stuff, but I haven't

seen him. I don't know what happened to him. Maybe his parents yanked him out of that school. Maybe he ran off. Maybe he's training with the Olympic swim team. Maybe he went back to wherever he came from.

It's been a couple years now, actually, and I'm still thinking about him.

Weird, huh? But the thing is, I really want to talk with him. Like, is his God a mother to him, or more like a sister, or kind of a girlfriend? How does he talk with Her? Like a buddy, like me'n Brent used to talk? Or better than that?

I haven't been to church since I was a little kid, but I'm kinda thinking about going back. I mean, if I can't talk to Julian, could I maybe talk with God? Would God listen? Could it be like Julian said, that God is alive and things might change? Could it be God doesn't want me to be scared of Her?

Gregory Maguire

He dreamed of burning Friendly's Ice Cream to the ground.

He woke up in a sweat. His alarm was pipping. As he showered, bits of the dream flashed up in his thoughts before disappearing down the drain. He knew that by the time he arrived to open up, he would have forgotten the charred roof, the flaming cases of decorated ice cream cakes.

"Mitchell," said Ma O'Shea, "for the love of Jaysus, out of the shower and drink your orange juice. It's half past already, and you'll be getting yourself fired for being late. Did you come home drunk and disorderly from visiting with your friends, that you're lollygagging around in there?"

Friends? What friends? Last night he'd been at the library, one of the only sanctuaries left for the poor or the unpopular. A perfect home for him since he seemed to be both.

She was a large old dried rind of a grandmother who had lost any concept of privacy. He scowled at her as he leaned around the edge of the curtain and snatched a towel from the rack. "Ma," he whispered hoarsely, "shut up—you'll wake the others. I'm not late yet and won't be? And I like to have the room to myself while I shave? If you don't actually mind?"

Old Irishwomen can really block a doorway when they want, and she stood there capably broad and immobile, folding her arms around her breasts as if she were afraid they would fly away of their own accord. "I've coffee in a jar and a couple of biscuits with jam for your lunch," she offered in a somewhat belligerent tone.

"They have coffee at Friendly's," he said. "That's what they *do.*"

"Don't you be drinking their coffee, or they'll fire you for draining the company dry."

He didn't answer. She finally turned and hobbled off down the hall. He shaved. What old-fashioned notions she had. She didn't understand perks. But wasn't *fired* a funny word for being let go from a job? Fired. He had dreamed of work, hadn't he? He couldn't remember.

The kitchen was suffused with a predawn, milky quiet. Ma stood in the unlit room, saving pennies by not turning on a forty-watt bulb, steadying herself with one hand on the bar stool. "You'll be able to take the Blessed Sacrament at the five-o'clock Mass at Our Lady's," she said. "I know you didn't go last night. Don't be late for the Gospel, or it doesn't count."

He snatched the paper bag. He knew it held a peanut butter jar of hot coffee, mixed already with milk and sugar. He didn't take sugar, but Ma O'Shea did, so that's how she made it. Every day, no matter what. "Thanks. Did you remember to leave out the sugar?" he said.

"Your muscles need sugar. It's good for what ails you. Now go on with you. Let me worry about getting your poor mother and her shiftless husband up in time for Mass." Ma O'Shea played the old Irish curmudgeon to the hilt, partly to amuse herself and partly out of conviction. She followed him onto the kitchen porch, watching her step. One hip replacement was enough. "I wouldn't take that worthless bike to work if I were you. It looks like junk, and so do you. I'd take shank's mare and be proud of it."

"Give me two thousand bucks for a used car and I'll, like, ditch the bike?" said Mitch, hopping on it.

"And don't forget your obligations!"

He careered the ancient Schwinn around the corner. When he was sure he was out of sight, he stopped and fished out the peanut butter jar. He dumped the coffee in the gutter and threw the biscuits in a hedge. But he kept the jar for returning to his grandmother that afternoon. She noticed the coming and going of household items; they were the tickets and tolls that proved her day was worth something.

His obligations. By that Ma meant *Mass.* Toe the line, pay your dues, keep the sacred account in the black, so when your other hip finally breaks and you pitch down the slope toward your death, you can approach Saint Peter with a grim pride in your endless obedience. Ma was public in her Catholicism, and she worried about not having handed down a strong enough version of it to her family. "I don't want to find myself alone in Heaven, ashamed at having my own issue sitting on some hot sofa far away in Hell," she'd say to her daughter and her son-in-law. "Get your lazy limbs to Mass and make an old lady happy."

Mitch had liked Mass when he was small, before he realized it was supposed to be something other than a show. When it was just music and candles and readings and communion, Mitch joined in: another kind of group sport, like baseball, like summer reading club. But when he was in middle school and began to learn he was supposed to be feeling something— to be saying something to God, silently—he began to feel tongue-tied inside.

He would sit in the pew remembering that when he was

little, his grandfather, Pa O'Shea, used to let him set up the crèche at Christmas. Mitch wanted to make the angels sing and the animals sing and the Wise Men talk. Play with them like action figures. "They aren't toys; they don't talk," said Pa. "Nobody gets to talk here, see, because it's holy."

"The priest talks in church," said Mitch, back when he liked to argue.

"He talks for us. We keep our big mouths shut or we get in trouble," said Pa.

Of course, now Pa's mouth was shut for good, thanks to a stroke; and thanks to the stroke, he never had to go to Mass. Ma had even stopped fretting over it. She just turned her zeal all the more fiercely on Mitch's parents and Mitch himself. She was a good solid layperson of the church, a capable agent of guilt. Thanks to her nagging, Mitch's mom hadn't been to Mass in months. "You're avoiding your obligations," said Ma every Sunday evening. "I won't be able to hold my head up in Heaven when my friends ask me what's keeping you. I won't know what to say."

"Tell them you told me to go to Hell, and for once I obeyed you," said Mitch's mom tiredly. "My *obligations*. Really. Mind your own fat business, Ma."

Mitch agreed with his mother, and when, infrequently, he chose to go to Mass, he made sure not to let his grandmother know. He didn't want her to think she was influential in any important way. He didn't want to give her the satisfaction.

Mitch was first at work, as usual. He unlocked the back door, flicked on the lights, carried his bike to the basement, and reached for a clean busboy's uniform. He liked the nerviness of changing at work. (It was the only thing he liked about work.) He liked the sense of trespassing on an adult world that, at eighteen, he didn't yet have full authorization to enter—he liked taking off his jeans and T-shirt and standing in nothing but white briefs in the middle of a semipublic space. Mrs. Honecki, who worked the grill, would arrive next, and then three high school girls from Plainfield Regional. They'd use this same dressing room. Would any of them think of him standing there almost naked?

He laughed, but hollowly, because he knew the answer. They didn't think about him at all.

He pulled on the baggy white trousers and the oversize white shirt. He felt like a small kid dressed in his dad's white pajamas. The pocket of his shirt had his name stitched on it in red, but nobody called him Mitch except for Mr. Paulson, the owner and manager of the franchise, and Mrs. Honecki.

On rainy days he took his lunch break in the changing room downstairs and ate his cheeseburger alone. At first he brought in reading for his college courses, but the breaks weren't really long enough to get into anything. Besides, it'd been hard to concentrate on college texts with the clothes of the waitresses hung sloppily in full view, and his own jeans and T-shirt there too. Though he didn't like the girls, he liked the way they looked, and he found the row of hooks with three sets of girls' clothing and one set of guy's an exciting thing to observe over lunch. (If it became too exciting, he stared at Mrs. Honecki's sweatshirt and stained overalls, hanging on a hanger off a hot-water pipe, and that usually altered his mood.)

On sunny days he went to the park across the street. It was a tired little patch of sunburned grass. The concrete ledges for sitting were covered over with loops of spray-painted vandalism. The only other visitor to the park was an old crazy guy with a misshaven face, a big sad nose lurching over lips that had fallen in due to his general toothlessness. The last papery shreds of his white hair were so clumped together by grunge that they lay on his scalp like a snipped fringe of wax paper. Frankly, he stank. He was too old to be a Vietnam vet with post-traumatic stress syndrome. He was ancient. He talked all day to the birds, when they came to get the crumbs he threw. But after the birds left, he talked to himself, the cars that sped past, the doggy-smelling bushes. He never much noticed Mitch.

One time Mitch left some saltines in cellophane near the loony's perch, for feeding the birds with. But the crackers just stayed there, untouched. The fellow carried on his one-sided conversation with gusts of zealous pleading interrupted by muttered curses or low mournful singing, in babbled sounds Mitch couldn't decipher as words. Who was the old codger talking to?

The public area of Friendly's was taken up by counters and booths. Waitresses buzzed around the central grill station, able to lean over the perimeter and take orders without leaving safe "employees only" space. At one end of the room ice cream cases were lined up below the take-out window. At the other end a side corridor led to the phone and the rest rooms. To prevent accidents with trays of food or dirty dishes, not one but two doors hung between the grill area and the kitchen. One swung in, one out.

The kitchen was Mitch's zone. An enormous place with a suspiciously antiseptic smell. Industrial dishwashers, deep steel sinks equipped with nozzles and spigots, metal counters lined with reverberating aluminum mixing bowls for tuna and egg salad. Adjacent to the pantries was the walk-in freezer, which held thirty-gallon cardboard barrels of back-up ice cream (more vanilla than anything else) and a dozen cartons of pre-formed square Friendly's burgers.

Mitch liked the kitchen because of the noise it could make. All those hard surfaces, the tile floor, the stainless-steel shelves, the roar of the industrial dishwasher, the clatter of sundae dishes and the swordplay of silverware cascading from the rack. There were several exhaust fans, and a radio he could turn on low, provided it couldn't be heard on the floor. The local AM station played the hits and plenty of commercials, and the banter of the deejays stood in for the talking Mitch wasn't expected to do. They spoke in huge letters, in slogans, the same key phrases every day, concluding every sales pitch with words that served as adhesive tape, static electricity, magnetic attraction, linking poor sad you to all the big wonderful things you could buy and therefore be: "THE SKY'S THE LIMIT. . . . BECAUSE COMFORT IS YOUR MIDDLE NAME. . . . GO FOR THE GOLD. . . . YOU DESERVE A BREAK TODAY."

The only time Mitch needed to talk at work, really, was to ask "What size?" or "Sprinkles on that?" or "Plain or sugar cone?" when he did the take-out window. He only did that when the floor was busy, and a waitress came smashing through one kitchen door saying, *"Window!"* and leaving in the same high-speed parabolic loop out the other door. When he'd taken the job in March, he had imagined that working at Friendly's would mean leaning against a counter, lazily wiping it down, while yakking a bit with customers. Listening to the wonderful verbal spatter that the job would tease out of you, show you that you had it in you to be hip, bantery, inconsequential. Whereas working at Friendly's really meant keeping your mouth closed, and he did.

Mitch's first assignment every day was to head out to the empty parking lot with a bucket of hot water and a toilet-bowl brush. He sloshed hot water on the ice cream stains on the pavement—small kids lost hold on their cones more often than not, and if Friendly's ever went out of business, it would be because Mitch always replaced the dropped cones free of charge.

Patches and dribbles of pink, green, white, and purple. The hot water loosened the ice cream, the toilet brush dislodged it, more water flooded it away. He was just finishing up near the handicapped parking when Mrs. Honecki arrived. She took two buses to get there and was always half asleep. "Hi-ya, Mitch," she called in too loud a voice. "You do good job! Good job!"

He brandished the toilet-bowl brush at her and kept his eyes on his work.

A long hard summer, this one. Hotter than usual, tedious, sweltery. But he didn't mind a break from school. The courses at the community college were boring but essential. Intro to Biology. Spanish II. Twentieth-Century European History (all the wars, the wars, the wars). The teachers were drab, committed, and exhausted. Most of the students either wanted to go away to school and couldn't afford it, like Mitch, or didn't want to go to school at all and slumped their way in the backseats, sleeping off hangovers.

Mitch had had a couple of pals in high school, but they'd been better qualified—by grades for scholarships, or by family finances—to manage room and board and go away to school. "Be glad we can afford this," his dad had said about Abanaki Community College. "Mitch, you get your two-year certificate, and then we'll see about sending you away to school. Just save your earnings, and we'll save too. Will two years more to hang around your hometown kill you?" *It might,* he said to himself.

But he kept his grades up, he moped about the library, and he worked evenings and weekends at Friendly's. He'd hoped his buddies would return home from college for the summer, but they stayed for extra courses, or took jobs on Cape Cod or at Lake George. Without anyone to pal around with, Mitch was finding the summer endless.

His main job was as busboy and dishwasher, but things didn't get busy until the second seating of breakfast regulars. So he loitered as he Windexed the front doors. He watched the waitresses arrive. They breezed past him without saying hi, like teen actresses on a soundstage, not even seeing the crew doing the setups for their big scenes.

"Hello?" he muttered, once they were enough past him not to hear. "Fine thank you, and you?"

Stalling, he finished up the plate-glass doors with an extra, third application of Windex. He'd come to think of the waitresses as interchangeable, and he no longer tried to engage them in conversation. They all went to Plainfield Regional; they were all in the same classes. They gossiped about their boyfriends and dissed their girl friends. If any of the waitresses had parents, teachers, or siblings, you'd never know it.

Today the employees' names were Mattie, Amy, and Caitlin. Through the left-hand kitchen door, the three girls came bubbling out on the floor, shrieking with laughter, untying one another's apron strings. Mitch couldn't hear, but he could see Mrs. Honecki mutter a tired remark. The girls pouted and made faces at her behind her back. She was busy buttering the cups for the first round of poached eggs and didn't notice, or pretended not to.

He couldn't put it off any longer. He went inside. "Oh look, it's Chatterbox," said Mattie or Amy or Caitlin. "Hi,

Chatterbox," they all chorused in a singsong voice. He didn't look at them and didn't answer as he made his exit from the floor into the steamy haven of the kitchen. "Hi, Chatterbox," they said, making a game out of it. "Chatterbox, you're my *guy!*" said one of them, convulsing the others. Oh, hilarity.

"Mitch the Chatterbox," said another.

"Chitch the Matterbox."

On it went. He turned on the radio to drown it out. "WHAT'S STOPPING YOU?" asked the deejay with compulsive seductiveness, hawking wares a mile a minute. "THE TWO MOST POWERFUL WORDS ARE *ME FIRST.*"

Mr. Paulson had told Mitch, "I hire the girls to be friendly. You, it's a waste of time to be conversational. I want you for the muscle you can apply to scooping ice cream and scouring pots and lifting the trays of dishes. And all the tips are pooled, so don't think you're being cheated out of your cut." As if Mitch only wanted to be nice because of tips.

So he had stopped being anything like friendly at the window, and before long he had pretty much stopped talking entirely. The girls in their Friendly's uniforms and aprons, their Board of Health regulation scary hairnets, had forgotten he could talk. He had heard them mutter the word *retard*. The waitresses ignored him so fully that one night he had dreamed that he actually *was* slow of mind. "Chocolate marshmallow," some pretty waitress was screaming at him, and he was leaning over three buckets of ice cream, pink, white, and green, and trying to guess which one might be chocolate marshmallow. Why couldn't he know? "Idiot at the ice cream counter," said the waitress, and her colleagues and the customers all laughed. In his anger he tried to find his voice to yell at her, but he couldn't make a sound, only a sort of soft-rimmed glottal choke.

Now he never did anything to persuade the waitresses that he was any more than moronic. Why bother? He was never promoted to the floor. He was never going to be a waiter. His job was hauling the plastic tubs of dirty dishes, flatware, and glasses to the kitchen and washing them; bleaching the coffee cups of stains every third day; restocking the crockery and flatware and ice cream dishes on their hospital-like aluminum shelves; and hauling the tubs of ice cream to the freezer case by the windows. Every couple of days he had to sign for boxes of lettuce and tomatoes delivered to the back door and cart them to the cooler. Grunt work indeed.

The girls yakked. How they yakked and yammered and yadda-yaddaed. They had perfected a brittle, high-charm manner, talking a bit too loud and fast, and very chummy— very friendly, more friendly than Friendly, even. The tone was identical, whether the shift was made up of Caitlin-Mattie-Amy or Mattie-Jennifer-Stephanie or Stephanie-Amy-Kimberly or Kimberly-Kyla-Jade. A three-headed split-bodied single entity of waitress. They talked over each other, through each other, finished each other's sentences, cut each other off. And never seemed to notice.

"And what can *we* get for *you* today," Caitlin would ring out, as if speaking for the whole flock of waitresses, whether the rest were working or not. There was an element of pretend in it, which Mitch found rude, but the customers either couldn't see through it or didn't mind. The customers placed their orders and handed back their laminated menus. "We'll be *right* back to freshen your coffee," Mattie rang out, acting as if she cared about keeping the coffee cup filled.

What they cared about was tips, and why not? That's why they were working—that and, maybe, companionship. You never saw one girl without two others. A bizarre hypocrisy of kindliness netted them all together. "What a beautiful baby; don't mind that spilled milk," Jade would say. "Pretty baby, as far as *we're* concerned, *you* can spill all the milk you *want.*"

Then Jade would swing through the kitchen door and see Kimberly or Jennifer hunting on the kitchen shelves for more pint cartons and lids, and Jade would hiss, "Catch the bug-eyed stinker at table seven, the ugliest thing ever to brown its

Pampers!" Kimberly or Jennifer would course out the swinging door onto the floor to take a quick peek, then veer right back into the kitchen through the other door, face rigid with restrained laughter. "Trailer park unmarried mom! Lock up the women's room! She'll stuff a roll of toilet paper in her pocketbook to take home as a souvenir!"

At first Mitch used to find a reason to go out on the floor within a few minutes. But he'd see that the ugly baby would be a normal baby, nothing wrong with it, and the mom merely looked tired and bleary. Did Jade really think the mom and the child lived in a trailer park? How could she tell?

But Jade didn't really think that. She and the others didn't really mean what they said. For them the floor wasn't a restaurant, it was a stage, and the customers served both as an audience for a performance piece ("The Friendly Way!") and as the unwitting foil for contemptuous improv humor. "Kitchen alert! Dyke sighting at table nine! All-girl bulletin: On your guard! Better send out Chatterbox! *He's* safe from her!"

"He's safe from everyone, since he's such a *Chat-ter-box*!"

No wonder he had dreamed—it just flashed back at him— of Friendly's going up in flames. What a temptation. Except there were few other places to get part-time employment, and he was saving every penny, every paycheck, every small envelope with one sixteenth of the week's tips, divided equally among all nine waitresses, the four cooks, the two busboys, and Mr. Paulson. Every scrap of change was going to buy him his own change, a change out of here, a change into adulthood.

"PAMPER YOURSELF," the radio urged. "YOU ONLY GO AROUND ONCE, SO GO FIRST-CLASS." He got the rack of clean drinking glasses out of the back door of the dishwasher—the racks slid in the front and out the back—and carted them onto the floor, imagining himself in a year. Confident, smooth of tongue, smooth of chin, a kindly light in his eyes. Knowing what he wanted to study, knowing there was a romance about to happen in some college dormitory room. Meeting bunches of friends at some upscale coffee shop, like a Starbucks! Making a clever remark (he didn't know what, he couldn't hear it in his mind, but he could imagine himself saying something incredibly, incredibly clever), basking in the bright, affectionate expressions on the faces of the very hip and good-looking friends he would finally deserve to have.

Life could be more than a sad cup of tepid coffee at a chain restaurant that was one notch above fast food when it came to food quality, and one notch below when it came to speed of delivery. A year from now . . . if he'd saved enough, if his parents could afford to help, if his grandmother kicked the bucket and left him a couple of thousand dollars' cash . . . a year from now he might be in his last couple of weeks of work here before leaving for junior year somewhere else.

The radio was really full of itself today, like Joan of Arc's voices telling him what to do. . . . "GET YOURSELF A LIFE," it said to him. He sipped at a cup of bitter, overbrewed coffee, thinking of his grandmother's efforts on his behalf. She got up early to make sure he heard his alarm. She'd made that coffee he had thrown out. It annoyed him to be so fussed over. She wanted to fuss, though. She cared about things in his life, like whether he went to church, or whether he'd be late for work, whether he'd lose his job. Maybe she knew how much he wanted the money so he could get out of here. More likely she was gripped by the specter of unemployment, like so many other people who had grown up during the Great Depression. Now he wished he'd kept her coffee and biscuits.

"Chatterbox," said Caitlin, "vomit on table nine. Lysol." She was in and out those doors, the words trailing behind her; she didn't look at him or even wait to hear any acknowledgment.

Mitch swallowed the coffee and reached for the Lysol in the cupboard.

The vomit, mercifully, was not much more than gassy water, more saliva than anything else, from a four-year-old who had been playing with a straw and a glass of 7-Up. "Noah," said his dad, who looked like a weekend-replacement parent, "does *Mommy* let you drink soda through your nose? If you're not going to behave, there's no more soda, and that's final." Noah glared at his ineffectual dad with a showdown look.

"Take these away, please," said Noah's dad, pushing pukey wet napkins at Mitch, not looking at him.

Mitch washed the bad smell off his hands with a special industrial-strength lemon soap. The Sunday routine was in full swing, but this morning was busier than most Sundays. He'd probably end up at the window today. On a hot day like this you could be scooping all afternoon if you got stuck there, which made your arm ache. Mitch always pretended not to notice when Mr. Paulson, scooping next to him during the busy periods, curled the ice cream shaving over itself to disguise an empty center. Mitch packed it thick and gave good value for money. He thought of himself as being appropriately Friendly.

He didn't go back on the floor again except when Caitlin or Mattie or Amy swung through and called, "Chatterbox, pickup two," which meant the basin of dirty breakfast dishes at station 2 was overflowing and the girls had no place to stash the crockery from the places they were clearing.

He enjoyed the swing of his routine, to the extent he

could, listening as much to the distant-waterfall roar of the air-conditioning unit as to the radio. Amy came in to look for some clean counter cloths. She hummed as she pawed through things, taking her time. Mattie winged in for a ketchup refill. "Can you believe those old bags at seven?" said Mattie to Amy. "They sat there for forty minutes and had three refills and left fifty cents' tip. Must be Jewish. They're still in the vestibule, futzing over who owes who how many pennies."

"Let me look," said Amy, and orbited out the door with a noncommittal expression. She was back in the other door a few seconds later. "Confirmed," she said, "total Jews." The buzzer for the take-out window sounded, and Mattie disappeared, the ketchup bottle in her hand to be deposited where it was needed along the way. Amy muttered, "Where are those clean counter wipes?" Mitch knew they were in a paper bag under the posted state regulations about complaint procedures in the event of employee discrimination. But since Amy wasn't asking him, exactly, he didn't tell her. Let her hunt.

She kept hunting. A moment later Mattie and Caitlin both came in. "Place is getting busy. Amy, hurry up," said Mattie. "Chatterbox, we need pickup at four."

"We'll make some tips today, then," said Amy.

"Are you kidding, everyone's jewing us today," said Mattie.

"If I've put more than five bucks in the tip till all morning, I'll eat five bucks' worth of matzoh balls," said Caitlin. They laughed, then all three of them left, Amy giving up on clean counter cloths and readying her order pad for prompt Friendly service.

Mitch made a louder clatter with the dishes. When he went to pick up at station 4, he glanced about the room. You couldn't tell that the clientele was more Jewish than usual, of course, or if so, which ones. And so what? It was just another meeting of the waitresses' gibe-of-the-moment club.

The girls kept up their commentary whenever there was a slack moment; they'd meet just inside the kitchen doors and fall against each other in helpless laughter. "See the gang at table nine! Total Jews!" shrieked Mattie.

The great comedy of it, sidesplitting, backbreaking. "But Mattie," wheezed Caitlin, gasping for breath, "they're nuns!"

"Thought they could disguise themselves," Mattie managed to get out, "but their secret is out! They've ordered only two tea bags for four cups of hot water! To save two bucks!"

Mrs. Honecki came in for a moment to make an emergency phone call and check on her sick aunt. The girls composed themselves while she was there, though Mrs. Honecki wore a big gold cross on her lapel and clearly was not Jewish. *It's that they think I'm imbecilic*, Mitch reminded himself.

What's to offend in me if I'm not capable of conversation?

Mrs. Honecki finished her call. As the cook she had no special authority over the waitresses, but she was older and a mother, and the girls tended glumly to mind her if she spoke to them. "If all five of us in kitchen at once, who's looking after cash drawer?" said Mrs. Honecki, and swept out to her grill. Mattie rolled her eyes and followed her.

Amy said, "We'll be lucky if we take in thirty bucks for the whole day."

"Not to worry," said Caitlin, "maybe one of us will get a doctor husband out of it. Flirt all you're worth, girl."

"My nose isn't big enough," said Amy. "I'd have to have a nose job."

"You, you don't have enough skin and bones on you for that kind of cosmetic surgery," said Caitlin. "Far too anorexic! You'll have to use something else for the added square inches of skin—like some lox, maybe—"

"You're talking inches? I'm talking added square feet," said Amy. "I want a nose you can plaster a billboard on. I want to sign my Christmas cards as Dr. and Mrs. Abe Honkerstein."

Mattie wheeled in the door and stage-whispered, "Jew alert! And guess who! The babbling old moron from the park across the street! You can smell him clear to the pay phones! Talk about your E.C.!"

"E.C.?" said Amy.

"Extermination Case!" said Mattie. She took in a few huge gasps of air, then made a show of holding her breath and pinching her nose, and dived back out to the floor.

The girls leaned against each other, helpless with laughter. Tears were streaming out their eyes. Mitch watched, with amazement, his own hands. They lifted out of the water. One hand headed toward the radio dial and switched off the big voice in the middle of some hysterical encouragement to "MAKE YOURSELF A—" The other hand dived into the sink used for soaking. It reached into the water and grabbed hold of a platter used for serving Friendly's lunch specials. Despite the soapiness, Mitch was grabbing it firmly, hauling it out of the suds, and he was bringing it down on the edge of the stainless-steel sink like a karate chop. The force was severe, and he felt it in his wrist. The sound was classic brawl-in-a-kitchen, a heart-stopping explosion of shattering porcelain.

Amy and Caitlin were startled and jumped apart. There was a silence from the crowd on the floor, and then nervous laughter out there, and louder talk to fill up the embarrassment.

"Oh," said Amy. She blinked at Mitch as if seeing him for the first time in weeks. "Oh, Chatterbox." She leaned forward, advanced a step. Caitlin, behind her, was biting her lower lip, though Mitch couldn't tell whether this was from real shock or an attempt to keep from continuing with terrible giggles.

"Chatterbox," said Amy. She remembered that Mitch was supposed to be stupid. "Chatterbox," she said loudly, as if he were deaf, "we're *so sorry*. We didn't mean to be *rude*. Chatterbox, I didn't *realize*—are *you* Jewish?"

She and Caitlin stared at Mitch as the door swung open and Mrs. Honecki came into the room to see what was wrong. "My grandmother," said Mitch, "who obviously I never knew? Died in a concentration camp in nineteen forty-four? And that guy in the park is, like, my grandfather?"

"Oh," said Amy. "Now I see."

Caitlin stared at the sound of a full sentence from the village idiot.

"And I have had it with all the nonsense," said Mitch, "and I don't care if it's the middle of my shift, frankly. So I quit."

Mrs. Honecki said, "Mitch, you don't do no such thing. You don't leave me in middle of lunch with no dishes. Please."

"I'll see you through the lunch rush then," said Mitch, "but everyone? Better stay out of my kitchen."

By two thirty he was already regretting what he'd done, but he didn't retract his glossy public statement. He went downstairs and changed out of his damp white uniform and tossed it in the laundry bin for the last time. He tore his name off the hook. He didn't say good-bye to Mrs. Honecki. He carried his bike up the back stairs and left. He wasn't sure if any of the girls saw him biking out through the parking lot to the road. He guessed that they were already making a new joke about him.

The old man wasn't in the park, either. He was off somewhere else, talking up a storm to nobody who would listen.

He didn't want to go home. They would ask why he was out of work early, and he didn't want to tell them. Jobs were hard to come by, and he'd blown it, somehow, with nothing to show for it but a pride at having stood up for somebody. But why did he do that? He didn't have an ounce of Jewish blood in his veins. His Italian grandparents were dead and buried in their Catholic grave. His Irish grandmother, Mary O'Mara O'Shea, was still alive, the resident sour conscience of his parents' home. Pa O'Shea was solidly alive, though stricken into oblivion at the Little Sisters of the Poor. So why had Mitch suddenly had it?

He wasn't going to go back to the college library. He didn't want to lurk around downtown either, in case his dad or mom saw him. He wouldn't know what to say.

Ma had reminded him that Mass was at five P.M. It was only three, or a little after, but he biked to Our Lady's and chained his bike to the fence by the parking lot. He expected to find the building locked, but the side door was propped open, and he could hear a racket, people setting up folding chairs downstairs, some parish finance committee meeting or something. He slipped inside and went heavily up the stairs to the church proper.

Mitch had no other understanding of prayer except as a kind of mental telepathy with God, but since human beings didn't seem to be wired to receive incoming calls—or since God had an unlisted number, or anyway He never answered—prayer had always seemed to him a kind of exercise in frustration.

That God didn't answer was no proof that God didn't exist, Mitch's seventh-grade religion teacher had said. He had grown a bit hot under the collar when Mitch had asked the question, but Mitch so rarely spoke in school that the teacher had seemed inclined to encourage him. The teacher had gone on: "Why expect God to speak to us in the language of science fiction—*telepathy*, for the love of Pete!—or, for that matter, English?"

"Because God is supposed to be, like, all-powerful and also kindly?" Mitch had answered. "And English is what I know."

"English is not the only language you know," said the teacher. "You also know something of the languages of signs and symbols, of gestures, of the natural world. God speaks to you in signs. And so you can speak to God in signs, too. And in actions. Not just in words."

The teacher went on with the party line: "Also, you know the language of the sacraments. God speaks to you in sacraments. If God is present in Holy Communion, then when you go to Mass and take communion, you're not just sending out distress signals at sea to a hidden lighthouse you can't prove is there. Jesus is *with you* in communion. That's what *communion* means—'togetherness.'"

Hoping to trip up the teacher, Mitch had looked up *communion* in the Merriam Webster's *Collegiate Dictionary*. The following week he had intended to score points with his friends by pointing out that one of the meanings of communion was "communication, intercourse." But he hadn't had the nerve to say *intercourse* out loud.

"Well, any kind of communication seems to scare you," said the guidance counselor when Mitch was in tenth grade. "You're not a bad kid, Mitch, and your grades are okay, so what's the deal?"

He wasn't mute. He talked some. He just wasn't a loudmouth chatterbox.

"Try praying," said the guidance counselor. (It was a Catholic high school.) "Don't forget: God will listen to anything."

If He'll listen to anything, there's no special privilege in getting His attention for anything I say, then, thought Mitch. *A hundred million yammerers in God's ear every day? And for what?* Since God wasn't exactly a chatterbox either.

So now, in church, he didn't know how to talk to God, if talking to God really was what prayer was about. Mitch just sat there instead, wanting to feel something, understand something, ask a question, receive a benediction, but he was unable to formulate the request in words.

The prettiness of churches, was that also a hollowness? Like a dollop of ice cream scooped falsely, to give the impression of density, of value for money? Mitch sat between slabs of colored glass, under ribs of varnished oak, looking at gilt-framed paintings and sleek modern carvings of saints and martyrs and the Holy Family.

Church was the real chatterbox. Four walls, a ceiling, and a floor, a box where people came to chatter to God. Why didn't God talk back?

Mitch said—he was talking to himself, he was, wasn't he?—*Give me a sign.*

And sat there.

And sat there.

Some moments later the side door opened and a figure entered, dipped a hand in the font of holy water, made the

Sign of the Cross, and crossed to the front of the church. It was Ma O'Shea, looking bedraggled in the August heat. She selected a pew near the door and sat there for a moment, fanning herself with a copy of the current missalette. She took out her rosary and began to tell her beads in an apparently perfunctory manner, occasionally glancing right or left, at the windows, at a sound of tires squealing in the parking lot. She usually went to morning Mass, so Mitch was surprised to see her there, and he didn't want to get up and leave, for the only open door seemed to be the side one, and he didn't want to pass her.

But after she had finished a round of prayers, she hoisted herself up on her knobbly legs and turned carefully. She made her way out of the pew and came back to him.

"I thought that was your bicycle," she said. "Work is so slow that you got off early? I hope they're not going to dock your pay or pocket your share of the tips."

"Actually," he said, "I quit?"

She sat down beside him, looking up at the altar, and said conversationally, and a bit roguishly, "Oh did you now."

"I did," he said, and told her what had happened. He didn't say he'd come into the church asking God for a sign. He didn't want to give his grandmother any ideas; she already thought she was on a mission to reform the world, starting with his family.

"The girls are fools," said Ma O'Shea when he had finished the story. "Girls usually are. They grow out of it. So, for that matter, are boys, and so are you. You're as much a fool as they are."

"I was making a point," he said.

"You lied, for no grandmother of yours ever died in a concentration camp," said Ma O'Shea. "And I'm not about to do so now just to make an honest man of you. I can't be bothered."

"You are no fool," he said, suddenly angry at her. "*You* know what happened to the Jews in World War Two. Some of the old women the girls were joking about, they were old enough to have had family members gassed to death? Or that smelly old guy? I don't know if any of them were Jewish, but they might have been. It might have been, like, *you* or Pa O'Shea in there they were joking about, even though you're Catholic?"

"Praise Jesus," intoned Ma O'Shea parenthetically.

"It's the principle of the thing? I'm sick of seeing everybody trashed."

"Then," said Ma O'Shea, "don't you trash yourself. It does no one any good. You get on your bike and go back to work. Maybe God put you there not to rage against those ignorant girls, like Jesus in the temple, but to teach them, like Himself with the little children." She straightened her backbone as if suddenly remembering she was being Jesus with the little children. She tried for something like kindness. It made her face look crooked, as if she were having gas pains from undercooked Friendly's breakfast sausage.

"You're too scared of poverty to want me to stand up for what's right," he said. "You'd rather me collaborate with small petty . . . idiots, so I can earn a buck. Your famous charity doesn't extend to someone in a different faith, does it?"

He had hurt her. Good: She didn't know everything. She blinked a few times at him and finally said, "The nerve of the boy! You'll understand when you've got bills to pay and a sick wife to support."

"I'm not going back to work," he said. "I'm going to stay here and go to Mass and take communion whether it means anything to me or not."

"We can agree on that. This is exactly when you should take the blessed wafer. The most important time for prayer is when you can't. The most important time to tell someone you love them is when you doubt it. It stiffens your resolve and reminds you what you intend."

"And what are you doing here?" he said. "It's hot to be out walking, and where's your cane?"

"I love your mother so much I had to get out of the house before I killed her. Your parents, they drive me to perdition," she said. "All that bickering of a Sunday morning! It wears me out." She sighed. It wasn't a bed of roses for her, either, he could see. She went on, "It's easier to care for those who are dead, or those who are far away. Frankly, I love my absent husband and my dead mother most, because they can't irritate the sweet bejaysus out of me the way your mother can. The hard work is in loving who's close at hand. The rule is 'love your neighbor as yourself.' Not the fellow on the other side of town, but your neighbor, the fellow who's in your face all the time. *That's* the hard work."

"We're all neighbors; that's the modern world," he said. "You can't make the distinctions anymore. You have to care about everyone. Catholics, Jews, everybody. Tell that to the friendly folks at Friendly's."

"Don't get sniffy with me. It's unappealing and rude besides."

"I hope you're not going to sit next to me at Mass," he said, trying to joke her into a better mood. "I'd hate to be seen consorting with my grandmother, as if that's the only company I can manage."

"I most certainly am going to sit right exactly here, as a penance, for you're not dressed for prayer, and it reflects badly on me. Jeans and a T-shirt in the house of God! You should be ashamed."

She positioned the beads around her wrist and began to

pray again. Opinionated, troubled, with a funny smell in this heat. He sat there thinking, God, is this the best you can do as a messenger?

In the morning Ma O'Shea woke him up.

"I'm not going," he said.

"You are," she said, "if I have to beat you on the bare behind to make you move. Get out of that mess of sheets and get moving. Your life isn't an episode on the television box, Mitch, with you delivering the loud brave last line and then slamming the door. You get up there and open the door again and go back and let them deal with you. Be a good example. Figure it out. You run away from this, you'll run away from everything."

She turned. "Besides, you need the money to go away to school. Don't think you're getting a penny from me until I'm dead and gone, and at that I might leave it to Our Lady's whole and entire, just to spite you."

He dragged himself through the shower. Ma O'Shea didn't kiss him good-bye this time, she just thrust his lunch sack at him. "What you do for others, you do for me," she said roughly. Mitch assumed she was quoting Jesus, but at this hour of the morning perhaps her martyr complex was kicking in stronger than usual and she actually meant herself.

The sky was lightening. Around the corner from the house he stopped as usual to dump out the coffee. But the peanut butter jar had no liquid in it, just a folded-up piece of paper. He took it out. In Ma's slow, wavery hand, there was a note.

About fifty years ago your grandfather ripped this out of a newspaper and gave it to me. Because he knew it would mean something to me. It did. It still does, even though <u>he's</u> lost his slippers and his pipe. . . . Stop thinking you're so alone. That's your problem. Love, Mary O. O'Shea.

There followed a painstakingly copied out poem. Ma didn't write very well anymore, so it must have taken her an hour to get this down on the page. He sat down on the curb and read it.

To a Jewish Friend, Wearing Green

For me, and not for Patrick, you have pinned on your lapel
The twisted ribbon shamrock that the five-and-ten stores sell.

I wear one for my mother, for her saints, and for her sires,
Who fled by night to Scottish coasts, and left the Ulster fires

And fields to follow God. And still, because in Palestine
Your mother heard the chronicle of Moses' myriad line,

The burning bush, the brooding in the strange Egyptian lands,
Today there is this clasping of our northern, southern hands.

O, the roads from Boyne and Jordan were bitter roads and long,
But a common gift of sorrow and a common weight of song

Made wonderful their journey, and our souls have learned to fare
From those sure souls who traveled it from Canaan and from Clare.

This day, then, be of Tara, and, small matter where you've been,
A hundred thousand welcomes for your wearing of the green—

A hundred thousand welcomes, dark-eyed child of Israel,
In your country's cordial idiom, I bid you—"Wear it well!"

Marie McAuliff
Published in The Washington Post,
Monday, April 3, 1946

Mitch didn't entirely get it. Who was speaking to him now? God? Ma O'Shea? His out-of-it grandfather at the Home? Or some poet who published something over fifty years ago about a friendship between an Irish person and a Jew? Or all of them?

There were no biscuits. There was a cheap shamrock made out of a twisted pipe cleaner, fixed with a pin on the back. He twisted the paper up and stuffed it in his back pocket, and fixed the shamrock to his T-shirt.

He didn't know about poetry. He supposed it wasn't unlike prayer, really, someone talking to the unknown. Some poet who didn't know that sometime in the future someone would be reading or hearing those very words, and making some sense of them. But spoke anyway, out of a need to speak, out of a hope to be honest. Out of a—what was it? He pulled out the paper to look at it again—"a common gift of sorrow and a common weight of song." Maybe that was as good a definition of prayer as any other: those common gifts.

He wheeled on. He supposed he could give the shamrock to the old guy in the blanket if he showed up. He could tack up the poem on the bulletin board next to the sign about reporting employee harassment. Maybe he could even tell the girls the truth: that he'd been lying, that he wasn't a tiny scrap Jewish.

"Then why would *you* speak up for them?" he imagined Amy saying. If the waitresses actually paused long enough to take it in, they'd all be embarrassed to realize he wasn't developmentally delayed. "Chatterbox? *Why?*"

He imagined being paralyzed into silence, as usual, by his inability to wrap all his concurrent impressions into one lacerating reply. Why speak up for the attacked? Because of the contempt in commercial radio come-ons, because of the insincerity of irony, because of the terrifying imprecision of prayer? Because—more simply said—we all have sorrow and song in common?

The familiar roof line of Friendly's came into view, at this hour a gray-purple silhouette hunched over a purple parking lot. He imagined the same old cat would get his tongue, as usual. He'd never be able to say aloud those complicated things. But those thoughts would be part of the answers, unspoken. And maybe God hears even unspoken prayers.

Virginia Euwer Wolff

RELIGION: FROM THE GREEK
RE LEGIOS, TO RE-LINK

I. Deborah: What Did Mary Say?

Dear God,

Is that actually your name? Or is it a name that got made up by people? Did you come down out of the sky one day and say, "My name is God"? And if you're the Father, Son, and Holy Ghost all at the same time, how do I know which one I'm talking to?

What am I going to do?

I've missed two periods.

Jason was so loving to me, I was sure I could tell him anything. I told him I was afraid I was pregnant, and I asked him what we should do. I was secretly sure we could get married and finish high school together.

He said he'd call me the next day and we'd talk about it. That was six weeks ago. He's avoided me ever since.

What if it's a boy? I don't know anything about raising a boy. What if it's a girl? How could I bring up a girl? I didn't watch while my parents were bringing me up; I didn't realize I'd have to know so soon.

Maybe I'm just nervous; maybe that's why I missed my periods. Is that it? Or maybe because I feel so guilty? But would that make me throw up?

I was ready to stop kissing him, but he kept on and I let him. Then I don't really know how it happened.

Well, that's not true. I do know how it happened.

Did you really suffer for my sins? I mean did one of the three of you? You didn't even know me. I wasn't even born yet. I wouldn't be born for another two thousand years. Suffer for my sins? I don't get it. Doesn't that remove all responsibility from me? If you already did the suffering by dying on the cross, then what do I do when I've sinned? I don't get it.

Maybe it was the movie's fault. We were watching a love movie. And the movie showed it all, I mean all. It looked so real, I guess I got confused and thought it was real. Well, maybe it didn't show it all. It showed almost all of it. Well, maybe not almost all. You know what I mean.

Well, it wasn't the movie's *fault*. But it was the movie's influence.

You know, God, praying was always so uncrucial to me before. It was so vague. I always said, Hi, God, please, God, thank you, God, have a nice day, God. Please let me get the prettiest doll for my birthday. Please have the orthodontist not hurt me more than I can stand. Thank you for helping me pass the geometry test. Please, God, let some boy like me, let some boy even love me? And then Jason appeared in the church youth group.

Did you actually *do* any of that, God?

I know a girl's body is a garden whose flowers are supposed to be picked only by her husband. Jason said we weren't going all the way. And then it hurt, and I said, "But no, stop, wait, no, please, no, stop. . . ."

And he said, "Just don't say anything. Just keep quiet."

If you brought Jason into my life, then are you also responsible for what happened? Where does your responsibility end and mine begin?

I don't even know the rules about you. I never felt you any more in church than out of church. You're everywhere, aren't you?

"Blessed are the poor in spirit." Matthew 5:3. Well, I'm poor in spirit. What shall I do, God?

Why won't you answer me?

Whatever I do is a bad decision: If I keep my baby, my whole life is rearranged. I'll always have to think what the baby needs before I think about what I need. And I'll be ashamed forever.

And if I give the baby up for adoption, she might get a bad home, with alcoholics or a father who hits or a sister who bullies. My baby would have a miserable life. And every day of my life I'll wonder what's happening with her, and I'll feel guilty. Or him. And I'll be ashamed forever.

And if I have an abortion, I'll go through the rest of my life remembering that I didn't give the baby any choice about living or dying. He would have turned out to have a life, the greatest gift we ever get. And I'd be killing him. Or her. How could I live knowing that? I'd be ashamed forever.

I have to sort out every detail, and I don't even know what all the details are. And make the right decision.

Girls have to think of details all the time. How many days to my period? Will I get my period in math class? Do I always have tampons in my purse, in all my purses? Do I have extra tampons in my locker? Do I always know where the nearest bathroom is?

Do boys think about details? I never met one who did.

"Do justice, love mercy, and walk humbly with God."

That's Micah 6:8. It's my favorite. But how can I know exactly what justice is with this baby? And if I do mercy, I'm kind to everybody. I can't be kind to everybody right now. I'm so mad at Jason for pretending the baby doesn't exist, there's absolutely no mercy in my heart for him. My parents are so moral, this will be such a shock, they might have heart attacks. And what's the kindest thing for the baby?

Walking humbly with God is what I think I'm doing right now. God, do you have any idea how humbled I am?

Well, of course you do. You know all my thoughts anyway, even before I think them. Don't you?

Shame, guilt, and fear. I feel like collapsing, not doing anything. I'm so nauseated in the mornings and so tired in the afternoons. And I'm so scared. Every Sunday I go to church wondering if my soul is breaking apart. Or do I have my soul confused with my heart?

I really thought Jason loved me. He didn't actually *say* so. But he was so loving. Was I really that wrong?

Here's another question, God: What did Mary say when the angel said to her, "You're going to have a baby and he's going to be the Messiah"? Wasn't she terrified?

If each child born is a manifestation of you, if every new baby is a miracle and a new chance for humanity, isn't that a good thing? But then why is it that for a baby not to have married parents is a bad thing?

Why in the world won't you EVER ANSWER ME?

If you won't answer me, if you won't give me some kind of clue, how do I even know you're there? Is prayer just shouting out into the darkness and hearing my own voice echoing back?

I wish I hadn't done it, God. I truly, truly do. I wake up every day and tell myself I have to abort this baby because no baby should have to be born if its mother isn't happy about it. By the time I go to bed that night, I know I can't do that, I can't undo this tiny life in me. Day after day after day. I've never suffered anything this bad before.

This is supposed to be teaching me something. I can't figure out in any way, in any way at all, what I am supposed to learn.

II. Zhandra: The Goose in the Bottle

Everyone suffers. *Dukkha.* Desire and craving are at the root of suffering. It is possible to go beyond suffering.

But I am expecting a baby. I didn't think this would happen. Does anyone ever think it will happen?

I take refuge in the Buddha.

I was trying to stay on the Eightfold Path, whose symbol is the eight-spoked wheel.

Right viewpoint is acceptance of suffering.
Right thinking leads to unselfishness.
Right speech prevents saying cruel things.
Right action means doing things that are creative,
    not harmful.
Right living is useful living.
Right effort enables us to let go of bad thoughts.
Right mindfulness means focusing on clarity.
Right concentration comes through meditation
    and brings peace.

Reciting these things helps me learn them. But is it a wheel or a straight path? These and other questions have baffled me from the start. I'm so bewildered.

I've been studying Buddhism for only one year, from the time when my parents moved our whole family into the ashram. I was angry and resistant at first, when they decided to sell our house and change our lives. They had been practicing Western Buddhists before moving here, but I had never given it much thought. They mostly let me just be, probably because I was young.

From the time we arrived, my mother and dad said they could feel the cold, materialistic world falling away. But I couldn't believe we were actually going to live here at the ashram, with its hand-me-down furniture, strangers of all ages, communal meals, rummage-sale cooking pots, and cluttered bathrooms. I was even homesick for the parts of our old life that used to bore me: dinner served on pretty plates, matching place mats, sparkling clean kitchen counters. I kept wondering how they could do this to my life. My dad accused me of sulking. I wasn't sulking, I was wondering.

The soft, sad sounds of wooden flute and monotonous hand drumming seemed to make things worse. The music that is always playing at the ashram sounded so gloomy, as if musicians were playing sleepily inside the walls.

Getting to know the five other teenagers who live here at the ashram with their families helped only a little bit. We all play basketball on the backyard court, boys and girls together. They've been friendly from the start, and we walk to the high school in a group. On the outside we look just like everyone else there. It wasn't completely embarrassing. Only somewhat.

But then along came Beni, in the midst of this group. I didn't especially notice him at first. It was Beni who began to explain to me that the Buddha really does live inside us, in the quiet. When I think of the Buddha's teachings, I hear them in Beni's voice in my mind. I keep telling myself the stories, trying to grasp the wisdom of the Buddha-Mind, the Middle Way.

Even the way Beni said the word *karma* was alluring. The Buddha found that we are born again and again, in the cycle of *samsara*, or "re-becoming." He taught that there isn't a soul, but there is karma, a life force caused by things we have done in previous lives. Our lives are imperfect. Only when we succeed in blowing out the fires of greed, hatred, and ignorance can we achieve nirvana, the end of imperfection. Some individuals achieve nirvana and don't have to be born again, but they choose to, to come back and help others. They are Bodhisattvas.

I thought Beni might be a Bodhisattva. He is able to practice nonattachment and allow himself to flow with the stream of life. In meditation he can sit in a full lotus position, empty his mind, and rise above all worries and problems of the world. He looks very beautiful and peaceful when he meditates.

Beni says we don't praise the mountains for being high. They just are. So must we just be. We are just a part of the dance of life. And he uses the special strainer of a monk to strain out insects from the water that we drink here. He honors all living things and will not kill even an imaginary insect by drinking it.

Can I honor all living things as much?

I even began to like the droning, wavy, floating music.

I told Beni I thought kissing was enough to show my love

for him. "Shush, shush, shush," he said softly.

I said to him, "But what will happen if . . . ?"

And he said again, so softly, "Shush, shush, shush, Be here now, Be here now. . . ."

And I am pregnant. I am here now. Now has changed. Now has changed again into now. Everything changes. Even my perception of change changes. As I have been thinking these thoughts, the baby inside me has changed. And I'm afraid.

Inside me is someone growing, not yet in possession of the power to choose. I have to choose for it. For him. Her. I hold the small ivory Buddha in my hand, and Buddha-energy radiates across the world.

Every time I get a whiff of the incense that is burned in the ashram, I have to run to the bathroom and throw up.

What to do? I keep almost telling my mother. Over and over again I nearly meet her eyes, and then I turn away before it comes spilling out. I need to get less confused first.

I'm trying not to let myself be attached to things. Attachment is distraction from the Buddha way. My thoughts of self are too restricting. I must learn not to think about self. But how can I help it when it's my self that contains this baby who is entirely dependent on me? When I try to meditate, this baby absorbs all my thoughts.

A Buddhist question goes like this: There is a goose in a large glass bottle. The goose is growing larger and must be released. How can it be freed without harming it or the bottle?

The Buddhist answer is: My thoughts put the goose in the bottle. Therefore my thoughts can release it.

Surprising bursts of enlightenment come when I least expect them. Maybe the goose in the bottle is just patiently waiting for me to catch on.

But that's just it: The goose is always in the bottle, without need for food or oxygen or future plans, merely waiting to be set free by the mind. Does it lie still like a picture of itself? This baby is nothing like that.

I spoke to Beni, telling him I've had the signs of being pregnant. He said I might be the mother of the Buddha. The energy of the universe echoes through the mother of the Buddha. He said I should just think of the river of life, flowing, flowing. Beni is very persuasive.

I'm not ready to be a mother yet. But could I refuse to be the mother of the Buddha?

I'm sixteen. I'm in high school. I wanted to go to college. I wanted to be a camp counselor this summer. I wanted to go to the prom with Beni.

I am supposed to think of myself as a leaf on a great tree.

It's a beautiful thought, but I can't see how it helps me.

I wish in my heart that I hadn't done it. But regret is harmful. Resentment is harmful. I am like a prayer flag waving in the breeze. Beni says not to worry about small, insignificant things.

The small, insignificant thing was his microscopic sperm fertilizing a microscopic egg inside me. I admit it causes me to worry enormously.

If I abort this baby, it will be like a magician closing the baby in its hand and then opening the hand, empty. The sound of the hand opening will never leave me.

If I keep this baby and it is a girl, she will live and grow and become pregnant with some boy who speaks softly to her. Or if the baby is a boy, he will grow big and say to the girl he loves, "Shush, shush, shush."

It's hard to imagine my baby having any previous life. It's very tempting to be possessive, to think my baby will be brand-new in the universe, crying for the first time. But of course that can't be true. We have all been here before. Haven't we? Who was I before? Who was this baby before? How can I practice nonattachment while this baby and I breathe together?

I need to develop imperturbable tranquillity.

I wish peace to all living beings.

It's good to feel the silence.

III. *Riva: A Company of Three*

La ilaha illa Llah. There is no god but God.

I wasn't looking for trouble when I met Ahmad. Even though we go to the same high school, we met by accident only after the dusk prayer. We met then several more times. He quoted poetry to me:

> *"We look to the starry sky*
> *And love storms in our hearts."*

These are the words of Mohammed Iqbal. Ahmad said them so beautifully, I began to hope he might someday ask my father to begin the marriage arrangement.

I was so stunned when he kissed me, but I was too enthralled to stop him. And later he said he was just doing a different kind of kissing. He said it was not what it was. I worried that we should stop right away.

"Be quiet, be quiet," he said. "Be quiet, hush. Hush." Although he whispered to me, it had the tone of command.

Allah teaches us that when a boy and a girl are alone together, Satan will join them, making a company of three. Why didn't I remember that?

In the United States it's hard to be a proper Muslim,

but I try. I have treasured the Qur'an. I've learned to pronounce complicated Arabic words; I can say *Qur'an al-majid*, "the glorious Qur'an," as well as others. I leave my shoes outside when I go with my mother to the women's enclosure of the mosque. I followed the slight fasting rules for children till I became old enough to fast at Ramadan. I haven't watched impure television. I've kept myself chaste, not letting my hair be uncovered, not letting boys see the shape of my body. I have hoped for paradise.

In submission to the will of God I have always tried to catch my hand and mouth, to prevent them from doing evil. I wash properly before praying. I have never eaten the meat of pigs or tasted any alcohol, not even vanilla. I've faced Mecca and prayed five times a day, although sometimes I've had to combine the noon and afternoon prayers when I had exams at school. Mecca is hard to imagine; it's so holy, and so far away, and even the climate and the religious air would be unfamiliar.

But while I was trying so hard to fast and pray properly, and to avoid the contamination of pork and the menace of alcohol, I wasn't even thinking about preparing myself for Ahmad and his sweet, sweet kisses.

I defiled myself when I stopped saying no to him. The signs of pregnancy are unmistakable. I'm a young girl, but I know that much.

I feel different in every way. But it isn't the exciting difference that I was told love would make. Love with a man is supposed to be splendid, thrilling. I am the opposite of thrilled. I feel I am on the edge of a precipice and I don't know if I should jump. I wish I could go back to that day and begin it over again. I would obey the laws of the Prophet (peace be upon him) and not even go near Ahmad. Never have I wished so hard for anything.

God forgives those who truly repent. But human beings are not so forgiving. One of the truths we have to learn is that reconciliation with people is more difficult than reconciliation with all-loving God.

No marriage can ever be arranged for me now. A girl is considered to be like a white dove. If a stain gets on her, she is ruined forever. I'll be useless, a broken vessel. People will say the word *whore*. My family's honor will be destroyed, and it will all be my fault.

These are the laws of Allah.

Living in its secret, dark pool down there, every morning the baby thrusts up my breakfast. I don't know what right food this baby wants.

I keep showing a brave face and pretending I'm the same as always. I pray as always, but each time my prayers are an emergency now.

I don't know how to be. This baby won't dawdle to give me time to figure out how to be.

When I spoke to Ahmad about the baby, he looked at me with frozen eyes and was quite speechless. I could see he was afraid. Then I didn't see him again. I asked his cousin, who told me that Ahmad and his family are moving away. He'll go to a different school, but she said she doesn't know exactly where.

The first word all babies hear is *Allah*. It is said first into the baby's right ear, and prayer to Most Merciful God begins the child's life. Will my baby and I be so unspeakable that no one will whisper this word?

The thing I wonder most is this: Does God know who I am? Does He know my heart is undefiled? Who would know the answer to such a question?

Ashaduan la ilaha illa Llah wa ashaduanna Muhammadun rasool Allah.

I bear witness that Allah is the one true God and Muhammad (peace be upon him) is His last messenger, the Seal of the Prophets.

In humility, O Lord, I await thy decision. Do thou not burden me beyond my strength to bear. Thou art the All-Knowing, All-Wise, Infinitely Just, and Most Merciful God.

Deborah: Not Always

Dear God,

When my mom saw me down on my knees beside my bed, praying, and then down on my knees in front of the toilet, puking, she figured it out instantly. She was appalled, hurt, angry, disappointed, and afraid. She took two days off from work to think it through. And she began to see that I felt the same things she did, but more so.

She and my dad talked about it for days, both loudly and softly, both to me and to each other. My dad stalked up the stairs, my mother cried in the bathroom. My dad slumped on the couch, my mom alphabetized the herbs and spices.

Little floating thing, getting everyone so excited, sorrowful, enraged. Everyone was terrified of a little tiny baby.

And then I found I wasn't. Not so much, anyway. My fear began to shrink. How did you help me do that, God?

And I told them: I'm going to have this baby, and our family will enlarge by one. Dear God, I'll need your help every single day. I have to count on you. I'll try to remember all the time what a blessing this baby is.

My mom and dad will survive. My mom said, "Well, I guess one of the things we get to do in the world now is love this baby." My dad put his arms around me for the first time in a week. He said, "We'll be okay. We'll be okay." It sounded as if he was more asking than announcing.

Will we be okay, God?

I think I won't always hurt this badly. Not always.

The next twenty years will be my hardest job of all. Help me.

Zhandra: The Sound of the Gong

A clear lake that is temporarily hidden in fog is still a clear lake.

When Beni walked through the common room whistling a little tune, I had a sudden thought: Between the fear that comes on me at all hours of the day or night and the unconcerned calmness in Beni's placid whistling, there is a way of right action. It is to be with this baby here and now, to give it my mindful attentiveness. I can try to apprehend the immeasurable mystery inside me, to envision its knees, ears, chin, the baby knuckles on the baby hands. A little more each day.

Every afternoon I read to the baby that it may know stories. Every evening I sing to it that it may know music. The sea accepts the dewdrop, but it is also said that the dewdrop opens to welcome the sea.

My parents have found out, of course. They are trying to

transform their disappointment into enlightened acceptance. My mother has hugged me and stroked my belly, saying, "Gentleness and balance, gentleness and balance." My father had a talk with Beni and then they shot baskets together on the backyard court. It didn't look very enlightened to me. They looked like ordinary men, dribbling and shooting. But what was I expecting? There was once a Zen master who was asked to tell the story of his life. He replied, "Just one mistake after another." The Buddha teaches that our most overwhelming questions are like the wind in the trees: We always notice them, but their answers are out of our grasp.

My parents were a bridge to the wife and husband in the ashram who want a baby so fervently and haven't been able to conceive one. They're the ones who will give this returning child a home. They are kind and loving, and have long wanted to be parents. They've been getting ready and hoping for a baby; I haven't done either one.

Until then, I'll keep this baby in its safe house, fed and rested well, cared for and sung to, until the doctor cuts the cord and we go our separate ways.

It's as if life were a vast tapestry continuously being woven, and each of us who is working on the weaving of it can see only the small, intricate stitches and knots of our own tiny section. We can't know the interweavings of the whole cloth.

Everyone suffers. *Dukkha.*

I treasure these months. As I separate from this baby, I will try to concentrate on asking: Where does the sound of the gong go after it's rung?

I will take refuge in the Buddha.

Riva: Allah Knows All Things

I have never been so shocked, never felt such pain, and never have seen so clearly God's presence and power. Allah loosened the baby's grip in me, and with His mighty strength and wisdom He swept the baby away. Its soul is in heaven with the all-loving God. "He sends down the rain, and it is He who knows the yet unborn" (Qur'an XXXI, verse 34).

I had not done anything out of the ordinary. Except in my mind and heart, where all was chaos for weeks and weeks. I ate as usual, went to my classes as usual, prayed as usual. And all the time the vomiting, too.

My shame will never go away, but Allah the All-knowing will guide me.

There was so much blood. I quickly scrubbed the steps, the carpet, the hallway, my clothing. I've tried to keep everyone from finding out, so my life will appear to be normal.

But I think my mother knows. She gives me looks, furtive

and secret. The air between us is weighted with unsaid things. At times she is sharp tongued, and at other times she suddenly embraces me. I keep the upheaval contained inside me, but we hold each other for a long, long time. She made a doctor's appointment, saying it was time for me to have a checkup. This was the first time she has been so interested in sending me for a checkup.

I hear my father, behind closed doors, demanding of my mother, "What is bothering you? Something must be bothering you." And she repeats, "Nothing. I told you, nothing." My father is a fragile man, burdened with business disappointments. He surely couldn't bear this distress.

Being a mother looks easy on the surface, but it must be the most mystifying occupation. It is always of full of surprises, a job for someone with huge understanding and constant prayerful consultation with God who knows all things.

Allah is All-comprehending,
         All-gracious,
              All-compassionate.

"There are two kinds of Jews . . ." Uncle Phil raised his index and middle fingers—a Pope-ish gesture that suited his pontificating.

"Ones with money and ones without," interrupted his older brother, Uncle Bob, imitating the gesture and turning it into a benediction.

Everyone at the table laughed, except for Natalie. She was staring out the dining-room window across the street. *Is it?* She watched the latest approaching car. *It isn't.* She gave a little twitch but didn't know if it was from disappointment or relief.

Even if she had been listening, she wouldn't have laughed. She'd heard this conversation before whenever The Uncles showed up for dinner, and she was tired of it. Phil used to be her favorite uncle before he got religious—before he married Aunt Arlene, orthodox, widowed, and with a teenage son. The funny thing was a few years ago Natalie might even have listened eagerly to these arguments. That was when she yelled at her parents in a restaurant because they were eating bread instead of matzoh during Passover; when she begged her mother to light the Sabbath candles because that was what Jewish women were supposed to do; when she told her dad he should stop working at his clothing store on Saturdays because it was against the Ten Commandments. She couldn't remember what brought on this spate of religiosity, or what ended it. But it was gone; good riddance, she told herself.

"There are observant Jews, Jews who follow the Torah . . ." Uncle Phil continued, glancing so obviously at his wife and stepson that everyone heard the words *like us* though he never said them. "And then there are Jews who believe that being Jewish is the same as being . . ." He stared at the yin-yang pendant Natalie was wearing. ". . . Chinese."

"But without the pork-fried rice," said Uncle Bob.

This time Aunt Arlene didn't join in the laughter. "There are plenty of Jewish pork eaters out there." She sniffed, also looking right at Natalie.

And plenty of Jewish pigs, too, Natalie might have said. But she was still too preoccupied to notice. Another car had just whizzed by. A bright-blue something. She decided she cared almost as little about cars as she did about Judaism.

"She's not a pork eater anymore. She's turned vegetarian," said Natalie's dad with equal disapproval, as if she'd converted to Catholicism or something just as heretical.

"There's nothing wrong with being a vegetarian," Cousin Aaron piped up. He was sixteen but looked twelve—and Natalie thought he acted that way, too. He tried to catch her eye and failed. She didn't want him as an ally—not since a few months ago, when he'd had a little too much Passover wine and tried to kiss her while they were looking for the *afikomen*—the hidden matzoh—under the pool table. "Come on. It's not like we're really related. Or that you have a *boyfriend*," he'd said. Threatening him with a cue hadn't worked; threatening to tell his parents had.

"You can be Jewish and vegetarian," he went on now.

"Sure, if Abraham had sacrificed a hunk of tofu instead of a goat, God would've been just as happy," said Uncle Bob.

"Would anybody like more cake?" asked Natalie's mom.

Uncle Bob blinked as if surprised that she was still there. Natalie actually turned and squinted at her normally chatty, opinionated mother. She hadn't spoken in nearly an hour. And hadn't she been wearing a different top earlier—one of her T-shirts with the odd sayings, instead of this drab beige blouse? Which tee was it? "I work best alone"? "Age and treachery will always overcome youth and beauty"? Natalie frowned. Her mother always changed when The Uncles came around—in more ways than one.

"They go to temple only on High Holy Days," Uncle Phil continued as if he hadn't even heard his sister. "They don't bother to keep the Sabbath. They might believe in God, but then again, they might not. What they really believe in is Woody Allen, or that new young guy—"

"Adam Sandler?" said Cousin Aaron. "He's really funny, isn't he, Nat?"

"Not hardly, Aar," Natalie muttered, still watching her mother. "I am Woman, hear me snore"? What *was* on that shirt? Natalie shrugged and turned back to the window.

"Yes. Him. They believe in comedians more than in God," said Uncle Phil.

"God *is* a comedian. He let *you* be born," said Uncle Bob, batting his big brown eyes, the ones that had gotten him a lot of girlfriends and lost him a couple of wives, in mock innocence.

"How about some more coffee, then?" asked Natalie's mother. "Natalie, go make some more coffee, will you?"

"No, thanks," Natalie said, craning her neck. A green Camry—the only model she'd learned to identify—was pulling into the driveway across the street. A blond boy got out of the backseat. *Is it? It is.* Natalie twitched right out of her chair. Kenny was home.

"'Scuse me," she said, heading for the door.

"Kids," she heard her dad humph behind her.

"Where are you going, Nat?" Cousin Aaron pleaded.

"Boyfriend," explained her mom, looking out the window.

"No way," said Cousin Aaron.

"Already?" said Uncle Phil.

"Finally," Natalie murmured, slamming the door on them all.

She waited on her driveway, watching Kenny and his mother unload groceries. He'd been living across the street for a couple of years now, but she'd barely paid attention to him until a few months ago. He'd been shooting hoops—badly—with his dad. Every time he missed a shot, he laughed. Natalie liked that. She had no use for serious athletes. They were as orthodox as Uncle Phil and Aunt Arlene, only their religion was sports.

She hoped that Kenny would linger on the stoop, and he did. Then she sauntered over. It was new, that saunter—as well as the sideways look she gave him. She looked at mostly everyone sideways these days, a mannerism that irritated her father enormously.

"Hi," she said.

"Hi," he replied, running a hand through his nice but a little too unruly hair. Everything about him was nice but a little too: His skin was a little too pink, his body a little too chubby, his personality a little too ordinary.

"What's up?" he asked.

"Nothing much. Family." She sat next to him and nodded at her house.

"Yeah." He nodded, too. "Hey, we might get a new car. A Land Cruiser."

Oh, God. Who cares? "That's cool," she said.

"Yeah."

Then they started to kiss.

He tasted like toothpaste. Peppermint toothpaste. *Why does he taste like toothpaste at five in the afternoon?* Natalie wondered. *And how come toothpaste is always peppermint? Peppermint or spearmint. Except that weird kind Nancy uses with the bee pollen or some other gunk in it . . .*

"Um." Kenny let out a little sigh. It made him sound like a dog having its stomach rubbed. *If I scratched his butt would he start kicking his leg, the way Sailor does?* Natalie nearly laughed. *Stop it. He's your* boyfriend. *You're kissing your* boyfriend. She gave a pleased little shiver at the reminder. They'd been going out just three weeks, but that was long enough for him to qualify. And if it wasn't, surely the way they were kissing was. *In public. Anyone could walk by. Anybody could see you.*

There were certain anybodies Natalie wished would notice. Kids from school who thought she was still the same geek who used to read books on improving your vocabulary, didn't need a bra, and once told the music teacher they were singing too many songs about Christmas and not enough about Hanukkah. Kids like Zena Riley and Kerry Christopher, who'd tell everybody who counted that Natalie Gerber had a boyfriend at last. But they weren't around. Nobody was around—except Natalie's family, watching, or trying not to watch, through the dining-room window.

Natalie squirmed a bit. *You used to be such a good girl,* she could imagine her father saying. *A good* Jewish *girl,* Uncle Phil would amend. *Who says I'm not one now?* Natalie told herself. *Isn't peppermint kosher?* She snorted. Kenny took it to mean he should kiss her harder.

For a moment she let him. *Is something kosher if you keep eating but don't enjoy tasting it?* "Huh?" She pulled back.

Cheeks flushed, eyes glazed, Kenny panted, "Sorry . . . I . . . sorry . . ."

Natalie sighed. *Dammit. He really* is *nice.* "'S okay," she said, looking at him sideways.

Then there was silence, broken only by the sounds of

sparrows arguing in the rhododendron and Kenny trying to catch his breath. Then Natalie, made restless by the quiet, said, "I heard they won't let Mr. Lupu chaperone the dance. One morning last week they found him smoking a joint in his car." It was a total rumor. Natalie knew it, and if Kenny had half a brain he'd know it, too. If he had half a brain, he'd also know it was time to ask Natalie to the dance. "It's the new millennium, *chica*," Nancy'd said. "If you want to go so bad, why don't you just ask him yourself?"

Natalie wasn't sure why she didn't. Was it because he might say no or because he might say yes?

Kenny inhaled and said, "Natalie, I wanted to ask you last week, but I wasn't sure . . ."

Here it comes. She felt a rush of relief. He was going to ask, she was going to say yes, and, see, Zena, Kerry, Cousin Aaron, Aunt Arlene, all's right with the world. She fiddled with the yin-yang necklace that Uncle Phil had eyed with distaste.

"But now it's okay. My parents said there'll be room after all. Cousin June's not coming, and she's already paid for. . . ."

Room? June? Paid for? Natalie was so confused, she squinted directly at Kenny. What was he talking about?

"So will you come to my bar mitzvah?"

"What?" Natalie said.

"My bar mitzvah. It's in two weeks."

A bar mitzvah? Nancy'd been to two already, but Natalie hadn't been to a single one yet. She hadn't even been to temple since the High Holy Days three years ago. She could barely remember what happened except for the shofar—the long, curved ram's horn. She didn't think they blew it at a bar mitzvah, though wouldn't it be an appropriate symbol for a boy becoming a man? She giggled. *I'm beginning to sound like Uncle Bob.*

Now it was Kenny's turn to look confused. She could see the beginnings of hurt in his eyes. *The dance is in three weeks. He could still ask me. I could wear the same dress to both. Zena and Kerry would never know. And it might be interesting. . . .* "Sure, I'll come."

"Great! Wait'll you hear me read my portion."

"I can't wait," said Natalie. She had no idea what he was talking about. *Gag me with a shofar,* she thought, looking down at her shoes. She was glad to see that one of her laces was untied. It gave her something to do.

Then she remembered. "A journey of a thousand miles starts with a . . . fabulous pair of shoes," she said.

"What?" asked Kenny.

"Something on Mom's shirt," she replied, looking across the street.

"I don't get it," he said.

She could've explained that it was a joke on an old saying that really ended with "a single step," but she felt suddenly, inexplicably annoyed. "Gotta go," she said. She got up. "Later." She took two steps toward her house, then turned and headed up the block to Nancy's.

"'The octopus is the most intelligent of all cephalopods. In one experiment an octopus learned to open a jar to get at the food inside.'" Natalie, peering over Nancy's shoulder, read aloud from the computer screen. Sailor, Nancy's standard poodle, thumped his pom-pommed tail. He seemed to find the information amusing. He seemed to find most things amusing.

"Why are you looking up octopuses?" Natalie didn't know why she bothered to ask. She already knew the answer.

"They're interesting," said Nancy. Nancy seemed to find most things interesting. It was a trait Natalie had always liked about her—one of many that had bound them together as the N-N Twins for so many years. "Saw one at the aquarium this morning."

"You went to the aquarium?" A few months ago Natalie would have known that. "What is this, you and your friend can't even take a crap without telling each other?" her dad had once groused when the girls had called each other a grand total of seven times in the space of two hours. Lately, though, she felt that Nancy didn't approve of her. She told herself that maybe her friend was just jealous. *I've got Kenny, and all she's got is Sailor.* But she had the uncomfortable suspicion it wasn't just that.

"Yeah. It was nice."

"I haven't been there in ages."

"You should go," Nancy said.

Natalie shrugged.

Nancy frowned and typed the word *chromatophores* into the search engine. Photos of bizarrely colored octopi soon filled the screen. *If Uncle Bob were here,* thought Natalie, *he'd see this as proof that God has a sense of humor.*

Then she said, with careful casualness, "So, what exactly happens at a bar mitzvah?"

"You stand up and sit down a lot," Nancy said flippantly. Then she turned around in her chair, narrowly missing clipping Natalie's knees, and looked quizzically at her friend. "Whose bar mitzvah?"

Natalie bent over and twisted one of Sailor's curls around her finger. "Kenny's," she said. "He just asked me."

"You gonna go?"

"Of course I'm gonna go," Natalie rapped out. Geez, maybe Zena and Kerry didn't know it, but Nancy did. "Why *wouldn't* I go? He's my *boyfriend.*"

"Yeah. That's right," Nancy replied flatly.

"I can't WAIT to go and hear him read his . . . his . . . *paragraph.* . . ." As soon as she said it, Natalie knew it was the wrong word.

But Nancy didn't laugh. "Portion," she said quietly.

". . . in the temple . . . under God's eyes," Natalie finished dramatically.

Nancy sighed. "I thought you hated going to temple."

"I never said that!" Natalie protested, somewhat loudly. She hadn't. She'd just said that it bored her. "Anyway, you don't even have to go to temple to be a good Jew." Her mother had said that—or something like it—after The Uncles' last visit.

"Is that what you think you are now?" Nancy muttered.

"What did you say?"

"Nothing," said Nancy, turning back to the octopi.

Later, on the way home, Natalie recalled that what her mother had actually said was, "Phil, who's there every single day and has his own *seat,* for God's sake, and Bob, who pretends he doesn't go, but he does a couple of times a month, I wanted to tell them, 'Going to temple won't make you a good Jew.'"

"Why didn't you?" Natalie had asked. "Why didn't you tell them?" Mom hadn't been able to reply.

Now she wondered, *Is that true, what Mom said? Going*

every day or every month or going at all? Going to temple doesn't mean you believe? Or going to temple doesn't make you good? What, Natalie wondered, did being a good Jew mean, in temple or out? She was sure her uncles would have plenty to say on the subject—not that she'd ask them—and anyway, Phil and his family were already gone, and Bob was just leaving.

"Chap Stick?" he offered, pulling one out of his pocket. Natalie bet he'd stuck around just to be able to make that joke. "Keeps those lips soft and smoochable," he added, in case she didn't get it—get what he and everyone had seen out the dining-room window. He kissed her on the forehead and walked out the door.

"That was some show you put on," her dad fumed.

"Who told you to watch?" Natalie said. It was the perfect exit line. Cool, calm, very adult. All her dad could say was a lame "Oh, very nice."

But she had to go on. Hot, loud, very age three. "Besides, it's not like we were *boinking.* We were kissing, that's all. There's nothing wrong with kissing my *boyfriend.* There'd be something wrong if I *didn't* kiss my *boyfriend.* We *love* each other. He just asked me to his bar mitzvah."

Natalie's mother, who'd come out from the kitchen where she was washing the dishes and trying to recover from her brothers' visit, said, "He did?"

"Yes. He did," Natalie said proudly.

"When is it?"

"In two weeks."

"Two weeks? Some relative or other probably can't come."

"So what?" yelled Natalie, which was *not* a good exit line, and she thumped up to her room.

It used to seem quite large, her room. But these days no room seemed large enough. Her computer was on. Maybe cyberspace would be big enough to contain her. Sometimes she went to the chat rooms, but never as herself. She, who'd never had a lead in a single school play, had a whole repertoire of characters. There was Jasmine, eighteen, runaway, lives in a commune, gets stoned all day long, and Dinah Mite, pro wrestler, wants to mop up the floor with every guy in the room. But her favorite was FloMama, the thirty-five-year-old woman with three kids who dispensed advice to the lovelorn. She told one guy to dump his girlfriend because she was cheating on him. She told another guy to stop cheating himself. So what if she was fooling them? They were probably lying, too. Everyone lied on the Internet. It was just a harmless little deception. Not all deception was evil. *Like telling Kenny it's cool about the new car,* she said to herself. *It makes him happy, right? You've got to keep your boyfriend happy.* The Ten Commandments didn't say, "Thou shalt not pretend," did they? Maybe she'd be

FloMama today. But first she'd see if she had any e-mail.

She did. A single note from Nancy. There was no message—just a blue hyperlink. It read: "Bar Mitzvah Basics." It might have been Nancy's way of being helpful or making up, but Natalie took it as another criticism, and she clicked the Delete button. But when the message came up asking her whether or not she really, really wanted to trash the mail, she changed her mind, hit Cancel, and went into the "Love Connection" room.

"**Hi, Flo,**" said Studmufn.

"**Hi, Stud,**" she typed.

"**S/A/L?**"

"**F/35/Alaska.**" Lie, lie, lie. She glanced out her window, which also faced Kenny's house. He was out on the driveway, washing his mom's car. Two girls were passing by. Natalie could recognize them by their contrasting hats, screaming pink and electric blue: Zena and Kerry. *Now they show up.*

She turned back to the computer and typed "**You?**"

Studmufn: "**M/26/Texas. But I like older women. Must be cold in Alaska.**"

FloMama: "**Frightfully.**"

Studmufn: "**Then you need some warming up, Sugar.**"

Natalie looked out the window again. The two girls were waving at Kenny, whom they barely knew. *They'll wave at anything with a Y chromosome,* Natalie thought. Kenny waved back. Natalie waited for the requisite surge of jealousy. It never came. *It's because I trust him,* she told herself. *He's only waving because he's nice.* Zena and Kerry waved again and sauntered off, deliberately wriggling their butts. "That's some show you're putting on," Natalie said aloud stuffily.

"**You still there, Flo?**" asked Studmufn.

"**No,**" Natalie typed. She left the chat and signed off the computer. A moment later she signed back on, retrieved Nancy's note, and clicked on the hyperlink.

She tried to scan the site quickly, expecting to discard most of the information as unimportant. All she needed to know was how to behave at Kenny's big event, how to praise his portion, which sounded vaguely dirty, but turned out to mean the part of the Torah he was going to read. Did it matter to her that a bar mitzvah boy could now be a witness in religious court or become a part of a *minyan*—the minimum number of worshipers needed to have a service—or that he was now required to uphold the six hundred and thirteen laws that governed orthodox Jewish behavior?

"Six hundred and thirteen!" she said out loud. How could anybody remember so many laws? Why would anybody want to? If you broke one law, were you a bad Jew? Two laws? Did it matter which laws, how many, or both? If you didn't know you were actually breaking a law because you didn't know it *was* a law in the first place, did that count? Did you have to know all the laws before the bar mitzvah ceremony, or you flunked?

But wait . . . apparently no ceremony was even required for a boy to become a bar mitzvah at age thirteen, a girl a bat mitzvah at age twelve. The bar mitzvah ceremony was a recent development, the bat mitzvah even more recent. A bat mitzvah. Neither she nor Nancy had considered having a bat mitzvah. And now it turned out that it didn't matter. "Hey, Aunt Arlene, I *am* a bat mitzvah!" she said aloud. "Yes, you pork eater, and just how many laws did you blow today?" She could practically hear her aunt sniff.

Enough of this. Her eyes were beginning to squint and her head to ache. "Bar Mitzvah Basics" indeed. She still didn't know what to do at the temple. She'd have to wing it and hope that she didn't embarrass herself and that Kenny, nice, nice Kenny, would still ask her to the dance. She grabbed the mouse, intending to get off the Web.

Then a tiny flicker on the screen caught her eye. Someone's name had popped up on her Buddy List— Aronic16. Cousin Aaron. She checked out where he was. A chat room: "Jews with Views." It figured. He'd never recognize her as Florence. She went to the room. Only four other people were there—unlike "Love Connection," where there'd been thirty-two.

Tallisboy: "so ur saying we're all good & we're all bad & the bad's in us all along?"

Jewly321: "How bad? Very bad or a little bad?"

Queen Esther20985: "Well, Luke, we don't all go over to the Dark Side. But we're all selfish. That's there from the start. And even the little lies we tell can mess up the world."

Tallisboy: "but bad can't be all bad, it comes from God, too, & u can't know good without knowing bad."

Jewly321: "How do we know what's good?"

Queen Esther20985: "Yetzer Tov."

Show-off, thought Natalie. But she waited to see if the Queen would translate. She did.

Queen Esther20985: "Inner voice. Conscience. Guiding spirit. It comes knocking when you're 12 or 13 and gives you the gift to choose the right or wrong path."

Some gift, Natalie thought. *Happy birthday—now you have to stop and think about every single thing you do. . . . What am I doing here? Why am I wasting my time with this stuff? Thanks a lot, Nancy.*

"What I want to know is," said Aronic16, "am I bad because I once tried to kiss my cousin who isn't even related to me?"

"Yes!" Natalie shouted, and immediately fled the room for "Love Connection," where she told Fat Papa that no matter how mammoth he was, there had to be some Skinny Mini out there who was dying to be engulfed by a whopping hunk of love.

Something was wrong with the air-conditioning. The temple was warm as a locker room, though fortunately less fragrant. Natalie vowed never to wear polyester again. Her mother had warned her the dress would make her schvitz. "I hardly ever sweat," she'd insisted, which was one of the reasons she'd be getting a D in gym.

It didn't help that the somewhat small sanctuary was packed. Kenny was not the only bar mitzvah. Relatives and friends of both boys, as well as the rest of the congregation, filled the pews. Natalie was wedged in between a thin old man who smelled of aftershave and tobacco and a plump young woman with a baby in her arms.

"If you come early, you'll get a good seat. Then you'll be able to see me," Kenny had suggested, blushing.

Natalie had nodded yes, sure, she'd be there before anybody else, but instead she'd come late—though not as late as the woman with the baby, who was, at that moment, trying to grab Natalie's hair.

She'd misunderstood Kenny at first and thought she'd be sitting with him, but no, he'd explained he'd be up on the *bimah*. And there he was, like an actor onstage waiting to speak his lines, in his blue suit with his white prayer shawl over his shoulders and a white yarmulke on his blond hair, which was slicked down and darker from some kind of gel or another. His pink face had gone even pinker from the heat and the excitement, and Natalie couldn't help thinking that some makeup artist should come out and powder over the sheen.

The baby reached for her hair again. *Who brings a baby to temple?* Natalie thought. There weren't even that many kids her own age there, though she was sure a lot more of them would show up at the party that evening. Didn't that make her a better friend, putting up with this god-awful heat and the closeness and the rabbi droning on and on in a language she didn't understand and suddenly wished she did, maybe it would make this whole thing less boring, but maybe not, and after all this, *Kenny DAMN well better ask me to that DAMN dance. . . . Oh, I'm sorry, God. I'm sorry.* It wasn't right to talk like that . . . to think like that? . . . in temple. *Why should temple be more important than any other place? Why shouldn't* any *place be as important as temple, damn-wise?*

What? There went her brain, having a mind of its own again. It seemed to be doing that too often these days . . . and nights. She couldn't even sleep lately for all that damn thinking. *Sorry, God. Sorry, sorry, sorry.*

Sweat beaded on her upper lip. She brushed it away. Her arm felt limp. Her head felt a bit too light.

Then, hands clenched, brow furrowed in concentration, Kenny rose and walked to the pulpit. *At last.* Natalie tried to smile encouragement, but it made her nervous, looking at him. Then she realized he wasn't looking at her either. He wasn't looking at anyone. Staring down at the Torah, he began to read, a bit haltingly at first, then more smoothly. His voice was pleasant, if a little too singsong. He didn't stumble. At least Natalie didn't think he did. She wished she knew what he was reading, was sorry she hadn't asked. Was it a tedious list of "begats" or her favorite, the story of Joseph the dreamer in the wonderful coat that was definitely not polyester? Did he know he didn't have to do this today, in front of so many people? Did he know he was already a bar mitzvah, no matter what? Did it make him feel good to stand up there, reading his portion . . . his *long* portion? Natalie almost giggled, and hiccuped instead. Did it make him more wise? More Jewish? More grown-up? Did he know, was he glad, that among all the gifts he'd get today, all the fountain pens and video games and new clothes and money, he now had the gift of choice?

He looked up then, finished at last, and smiled—first

with relief, then with obvious pride at his mother, his father, his grandparents and sisters, all in the front row. Still smiling, he scanned the room, and Natalie knew he was looking for her. She glanced sideways, glanced back. When he caught her eye, she smiled back. His smile widened in genuine pleasure. It made her eyes sting.

"Page five eighty-two," said the rabbi, gesturing for the congregation to rise. The old man next to her rustled the pages in his prayer book. Natalie grabbed hers from the back of the bench in front of her, and stood, fumbling through the worn text, which was in English as well as Hebrew, but the words seemed to be swimming. The word *choice* seemed to be doing the crawl from page to page. It made her woozy.

They sat and rose, sat and rose again. Sweat began to seep down into her bra. Her dress clung like a scuba diver's wet suit. She looked up at the Eternal Light over the Ark, the cabinet where the Torah was housed when not in use. It seemed to swell and glare, relentless as a desert sun. The baby next to her grunted. A stench slowly rose from his diaper. Natalie gagged and, holding her hand over her nose and mouth, pushed out of the pew, up the aisle, and out the door.

In the ladies' room she hurried to a sink, turned on the tap, and rubbed handful after handful of cold water on her face. A few moments later, as she was leaning against the wall taking careful breaths and thinking that the smell, or its memory, was finally gone, the mother and baby hustled into the room.

"Ooh, stinky baby. Stinky, stinky baby," the woman half apologized, half cooed.

I can't believe this, Natalie thought. She couldn't stay in here. But she wasn't ready to go back into the sanctuary. Leaning awkwardly against the sink, she watched in disgust and fascination as the woman, with practiced hands, plunked the baby on the changing table, unsnapped his romper, pulled off the soiled diaper, wrapped it in a plastic bag, and dumped it in the bin. "Whose are you here for?" the woman asked, cleaning the baby's bottom.

It took a moment for Natalie to realize what she was asking. "Oh. Kenny. Kenny Platsky."

"Ah. I don't know him, but he did a nice job." She pulled out a fresh diaper and slid it under her son. "He your boyfriend?"

Sure. Of course. Who am I kidding? Just yourself, baby, that's what FloMama would say. You know Flo, little older than you, with three kids? Or Jasmine or Dinah Mite? Then there's Natalie Gerber. You know her? Lies a lot, cheats a little, doesn't steal. . . . Aww, damn, what business is it of yours, anyway? Natalie stood there, saying nothing, watching the baby, who was laughing as if he were in on some colossal joke.

And then she felt as though she'd been tapped gently on her forehead, and her heart seemed to tilt ever so slightly sideways as if something had just tiptoed inside.

"None of my business, right?" said his mother.

Natalie looked straight on into the woman's open, freckled face and made a choice. "No," she said. "No, he's not my boyfriend."

"Oh. Oh, well."

"He . . . used to be . . . but he was more into it than I was."

"Hmmm. I had one like that years ago."

"It was kind of . . . my fault. . . . I sort of used him, you know? . . . And I've been thinking maybe God's mad at me?" She didn't know why she said that, and to this total stranger— or was it her gurgling kid? A single tear ran down her cheek. She brushed it away before the woman saw it.

"He'll get over it," the woman replied, snapping the baby's suit closed. Natalie didn't know if the woman meant God or Kenny or maybe both. She gave her son a kiss on his tummy. "There; now you smell a whole lot better," she said, and crossed to the sinks. Natalie moved over to give her room. The woman washed her hands carefully, then glanced down at Natalie's suede sandals. "Hey, fabulous shoes," she said.

Scooping up her baby, she smiled and walked out of the room.

Natalie looked down at her feet and laughed or cried or maybe both.

The moon jellies were drifting around the tank like animate dandelion puffs. *Right now, Uncle Phil, Aunt Arlene, and Cousin Aaron are in temple,* Natalie told herself. *Uncle Bob is probably having brunch with his latest girlfriend. Dad's mowing the lawn. Zena and Kerry are doing each other's nails and talking, talking, talking about the dance tonight. And Kenny . . .*

Natalie sighed. It had been hard breaking up with him. At first she thought she wouldn't have to say a thing; she'd just stop talking on the phone, stop coming over, stop kissing, for God's sake. She didn't bank on Kenny coming to *her* house and asking, "What's going on?" He didn't get it at first. He thought he'd done something wrong. Was it because he hadn't asked her to the dance? He should've explained—he had another bar mitzvah to go to. He had bar mitzvahs to go to for the next three weeks.

No, it wasn't that, Natalie had to tell him. But what was it? She couldn't say he'd never really been her type in the first place. What was her type? She couldn't say he was too nice for her. God knew what that might make him do to the next girl he dated. In the end she just said she realized she didn't want to go out with anybody right now. She had to figure out what she wanted from herself first. Which was at least true, if not the whole story.

"They're so fantastic, aren't they?" Nancy said, studying the moon jellies. She hadn't minded at all going to the aquarium so soon after her last visit. Natalie's mom hadn't minded taking them, either.

"Yes, they are," Natalie agreed.

"That's how I know God exists," said Nancy.

"From moon jellies?"

"Sure. They look so divine."

"You know, there's a Jewish prayer you're supposed to say when you see a beautiful tree or something like that," said Natalie.

"Yeah? How'd you know that?" asked Nancy, turning to her.

"Saw it in the prayer book at Kenny's bar mitzvah," Natalie said, suddenly feeling a bit shy. It was the one prayer that had caught her attention when she'd gone back into the sanctuary after her trip to the toilet.

"That's nice."

"I don't say it, though," Natalie added quickly. She didn't—it was enough to know it was there.

"You girls still looking at the jellyfish?" said Natalie's

mother, who'd already been up and down the exhibit twice. She had on a new T-shirt that said, "In all of history, no one has ever died of laughter." Natalie had told her to wear it the next time The Uncles came. "You really think so?" her mother had asked. "Yes. Yes, I do," Natalie answered firmly. "I just might," her mother had replied.

"You know, people think God created men and women in His image," said Nancy. "But I think God created moon jellies in His image . . . and starfish and walruses and flamingos and palm trees—"

"And poodles?" Natalie was laughing.

"Definitely poodles."

"Not a very Jewish idea," said Natalie.

"Yes, what would Phil say about that? There are *two kinds of Jews*," said her mother, with a wicked imitation that startled and tickled Natalie.

"Oh, there are a lot more kinds than that," said Nancy.

As they strolled over to look at the octopi, Natalie decided there was a good chance that Nancy was right.

ON EARTH   *Jacqueline Woodson*

It is July when the letter comes from my mother. The letter is part of Jehovah's plan, we know, but still it silences us.

Although I miss you all terribly, the letter says, *I am not ready for you to come home.*

We sit at my grandmother's feet on the front porch stairs while yellowjackets and butterflies circle around us and the porch swing whines and creaks with her rocking. My sister, Layana, is fifteen and has taken on a faraway look this summer. She is walking the wide road, Layana is. The one that can only lead to destruction. She prays with her eyes open. Her head unbowed. When my grandmother reads the part about my mother needing more time, Lay turns and stares off into the distance, her eyes closing into slits. We have been at my grandmother's house since March, when Layana found my mother huddled and crying on the floor of our apartment in New York City. *A nervous disorder,* the doctors said. *Complicated by a hormonal imbalance.*

She went crazy, Layana said. *Simple as that.*

It is almost a blur now—my mother huddled in the corner speaking a language that wasn't a language, whispering words that weren't words, the ambulance screaming down our street, my friends running to our front stoop and asking in whispers, "What happened?" Then the four of us in a room somewhere, bright fluorescent lights above us and a woman asking questions about our next of kin. A day later my grandmother was standing in the doorway saying, *You all will have to come stay with me for a while.* And me and the twins running into her arms, but Layana holding back, looking everywhere but at the four of us.

March seems like a long time ago.

Layana blinks, then rubs her eyes and frowns. She has pulled her thick hair back into a braid and sits chewing the end of it. Layana is the beautiful one, people say. She is tall and narrow, with Mama's dark eyes and thick lashes. Last summer, when we were visiting our grandmother and the relatives came, they turned Lay this way and that, saying *Let me look at you. Girl, you are surely Carletta's child. Got all her pretty, didn't you?*

Gonna break hearts if you ain't already. But now when the relatives come, Layana leaves. You look right, you see their cars pulling in. You look left, you see Layana taking off down the road, her thin linen dress blowing slow in the breeze, her thick black braid bouncing soft between her shoulder blades. *Maybe I got all her crazy too,* Layana whispers at night. *Some nights I ask Jehovah to take it all away. You're lucky, Carlene. You probably didn't inherit anything from her.* And it's true. I am not pretty like Layana. My nose is too narrow and my cheekbones jut up out of my face too fiercely. My eyes and hair are the same brown as my skin, so that when you stand looking at me, it's hard to tell where skin stops and hair begins. Even my name, although it sounds like my mother's, has nothing to do with her. I was named for the way I was born—inside the back of my father's Mustang—a black convertible he got into two years later and kept on driving.

Now Layana glares down the road as my grandmother reads our mother's letter.

The doctors say I need more time alone.

The road is red dirt and curves at the end of our property onto a wider, paved one. That paved road keeps going, getting wider and wider until you're finally in Charleston, South Carolina. Charleston's our big city, but my grandmother tells us Anderson is growing, says soon this town will be a big city town like Charleston. My grandmother's southern accent is heavy. She has lived in Anderson all of her life. When we ride the bus, she herds us all four to the very back. "It's what I know," she says when Layana reminds her that the laws changed a long time ago. "It's a law that stayed in my bones."

Like God.

"The first time I walked into a Kingdom Hall," our grandmother tells us, "I knew I was home."

"How?" Layana asks. "You going to tell us God came down into the Hall and called your name?"

"He didn't have to," she says, ignoring Layana's sarcasm. "I had already called his. 'Jehovah,' I said. 'Jehovah God.'"

"How old was Mama?" I ask again, because I've heard this story and asked this question so many times.

"Twelve," my brother Clay says. "Twelve twelve twelve."

"Did she call Jehovah's name too?"

Layana glares at me, but I just go on resting my head on my knees waiting for an answer.

"Has she *ever*?" Layana says.

"When she was a child, she believed like y'all do," our grandmother says.

I look up at the sky. It is blue and nearly cloudless. Jehovah is up in that blue. Sitting on a throne looking down at us. Looking right straight through to our marrow.

• • •

At night, Layana makes me practice. "Say 'I think so,'" she whispers. "Don't say 'I reckon.' Say 'you' not 'y'all.' You want to lose all your city?" And I shake my head because my city is the only thing I have left. And the silver ring my mother gave me for my twelfth birthday. But as my grandmother reads, I feel my city slipping away from me. The cracks in the sidewalk in front of our building are fading. The double Dutch games and running to the corner store for potato chips and cream soda are almost gone. My mother leaning out the window to call us in for dinner is all whispery and blurred. New York is becoming a dream I used to have.

Way off I can hear my sometime friends Cora and Lubell singing "Miss Lucy Had a Baby." My big brothers are playing with the cuffs of their pants. They're both thirteen, born a minute apart and identical. Clay has a mole above his right eye, and Scott has one right where his thumb meets the rest of his hand. Otherwise, if you're not related to them, it's hard to tell who's who. Clay is quiet, and Scott is the one who can sing.

I swallow and stare toward the sun, not right at it because I know that will make me go blind but sort of sideways and at the edges of it, where orange and red meet the darkening sky. Soon the sun will drop down and disappear and it will be night. My mother has done this. Dropped down and disappeared. I twirl the silver ring. There are blackbirds etched into it, circling. *My mother is a blackbird. And we're four hatchlings. Without wings.*

Give the kids hugs for me and tell them how much I love them. Tell them, Jehovah's will, they'll be home by September. Tell Carlene not to worry. I know how she worries.

"I'm not worrying," I say, watching my grandmother fold the letter over and over itself. Watching my mother disappear.

"Your face is all bunched up," Scott says. "Look at your eyebrows. They're all knitted."

Clay looks at me and frowns.

"I'm not worrying," I say again.

Armageddon is what will claim the ones who don't believe in Jehovah. Fire falling from the sky, floods, famine, and plagues. If you try to hide in the water, poisonous snakes will be there to bite you. If you hide beneath your bed, God's hand will pull you from your hiding place and strike you dead. There is no place you can go on Earth and be saved. No place but into the heart of God. I stand up straight inside His heart, say my prayers, don't curse or disrespect anyone. I walk a narrow path. The hardest kind to walk. "Believe in Jehovah's will," my grandmother says, "and everything will work out in the end." I bite my bottom lip hard, close my eyes, and try to believe I will see my mother again.

My grandmother tells us to stand up, and we do, one behind the other with Layana last, so she can hug us for Mama. When she gets to Layana, she hugs extra long and hard, but Layana puts her arms out, keeping our grand-mother's hug from our mother at a distance.

My grandmother sighs. "You all go on and get ready now. A letter from your mama don't mean we got to be late for the Meeting." She sits on the porch rocking, staring off down the road. And rocking.

Scott holds the screen door open until we are all inside. "She can keep New York," he whispers to us. "Anderson got schools and stuff."

"Anderson got a girl named Lori," Clay says, punching Scott in the arm. "Got you with your lips on hers all evening."

Scott punches him back. "I ain't studying no Lori."

"You more than studying her."

"You keep kissing on country girls and talking like that, you're going to lose your city," I say. But Scott and Clay just look at me.

"You worry too much," Clay says.

I try not to think about my mother's letter as I pull a flowered dress over my head. I listen to the porch swing. When it stops, I hear the faint sound of paper and wonder if my grandmother is unfolding the letter or balling it up to throw away. Until this day the only leaving I have known is through death. My grandfather's death years and years ago. I know tears for the dying and a body being put into the ground. I know my grandfather's soft brown hands folded across his chest and his face, contorted in pain for months, at rest. I know how a disease sometimes wins in the end. Takes a person away.

Some mornings when I'm sitting with Cora and Lubell on the front porch stairs, Cora asks what's it like to not have a mama around, and I shrug and say I miss the smell of her, that's all. But that's everything. And Cora and Lubell frown and shake their heads at me. They think I'm a strange city girl, exotic as the pictures they've seen of birds of paradise but nothing they'd ever want to be or get too near. *You're all brown,* they say when they want to be mean. *Head to toe brown like swamp water.* And then days go by without us speaking.

The house is hushed and solemn. My grandmother has put a record on—Witness songs. We have always been Jehovah's Witnesses. It will be the religion of my own children if I ever have any. If the world doesn't end before I am married. My mother is no longer a Witness. Two years ago she was excommunicated because she was dating a man who was not in the Truth—our religion. The true one. A worldly man, the elders said. A man who smoked and drank and spent the night at our house sometimes. His name was Luther, and he taught me how to play chess and cornrow my own hair. At night I lay in bed imagining the day they'd marry—Luther in a black tux, my mother in a blue dress, and me following down the aisle behind them sprinkling white rose petals. But it didn't happen.

Tell them, my grandmother warned my mother. *Tell the elders about him.* But my mother refused to. So that fall, when my grandmother made the trip to New York to return us to our mother, she visited our congregation and had a talk with the elders.

Don't come to New York again, my mother said.

And my grandmother didn't.

Until last March.

My mother doesn't call. She is afraid of my grandmother's voice. Afraid of the damage one voice can do.

Technically, we are not allowed to speak to our mother. It is against the religion. But it is against the Ten Commandments not to honor her. "Honor thy father and thy mother," the Commandments tell us. Jehovah's Witnesses are the chosen people. Cora and Lubell will be destroyed when God sees fit to put an end to this system of things. My mother will be destroyed. *Our Father who art in Heaven. Please see fit to spare her.* But the Witnesses will be part of a New World, God's second Garden of Eden. The elders refer to it as Paradise on Earth. Even the dead ones, my grandmother promises, will be resurrected.

Every Monday we sit in my grandmother's living room for Bible study. And Thursday night we go to the Kingdom Hall for Ministry School. We will all go into the ministry once we are done with high school. When Layana says she might want to go to college, my grandmother tells her not to be a fool, and Layana presses her lips closed with the words still swimming around behind them. In New York we had our Bible studies with an elder from our congregation there. When he arrived, he and my mother didn't speak. "Get your Bibles," our mother would say as she retreated upstairs. Soon we could hear music wafting down; soft, sad music that my mother always listened to.

To be welcomed back into the religion, my mother was supposed to sit in on every Meeting with us—Bible studies, Ministry School, and our Sunday Watchtower Study. But she didn't. If she had, she would not have been allowed to speak to anyone, nor would anyone have been allowed to speak to her. *I wouldn't be able to stand it,* she said. *Walking into that Meeting and having everyone turn away from me.*

But you'll never be a Witness again, Mama, I pleaded the first time my mother turned to retreat upstairs. *And you'll be destroyed in Armageddon.*

Don't worry, Carlene. Jehovah has a plan for us all.

As I watched my mother disappear up those stairs, as I

watched her beautiful back sway heavenward, up into the dying light of evening coming in through the sky window, I knew she was slipping away from God even as she walked toward him. I knew she was slipping away from me. Even as she called my name.

What is Jehovah God's plan? the elder asked while Mama's music played upstairs.

There will come an end to this system of things, I said. *Death and suffering will be no more. Nor will wrongdoing.* As my mother's music took a seat on one side of me. And God on the other.

The elder smiled and nodded. Pleased.

We know right from wrong. We know we are special—God's chosen people. When the color guards at school raise the flag, we leave the room. We pledge allegiance only to God. We do not celebrate birthdays or Christmas because these are worldly ways, and although we are in this world, the elders tell us, we are not of it. I will never curse or drink. I will never dance or play Spin the Bottle. I will never learn the hand movements of worldly games like Miss Lucy Had a Baby and Miss Mary Mack. My brothers will never go to war. One day, we are promised, we will have happiness and life everlasting.

One day.

• • •

It is almost evening when we leave the house, Layana and me in dresses, our hair unbraided, brushed, and oiled, Clay and Scott in shirts and ties. Our grandmother behind us wearing a soft blue dress and navy beads. As we climb into her car and drive to our Meeting, Layana sits in the front seat beside our grandmother and sighs. Even after all these years, the car still smells of my grandfather's pipe, the one he was never allowed to smoke in the house, smells of the tobacco that is against our religion. But the elders didn't know he smoked. No one ever told them. I stare at the back of my grandmother's head, at the gray curls pulled to the top of her head, at the straight neck and shoulders. She is proud of her holiness. Proud of the good Witnesses she and her grandchildren have become. There is no room on the narrow road for smoking or worldly men. There is so much room at its edges for hypocrisy.

Layana rolls the window down and sticks her head out. Three years from now she will be gone, down that road and off into the foggy light of morning, her suitcase banging against her leg, her acceptance letter to Swarthmore folded up inside her knapsack. And for months I will wake to find her gone and cry.

Beside me Clay and Scott play scissors, paper, rock, Scott singing the words softly over and over again—"Scissors, paper, rock, scissors, paper, rock, scissors, paper, rock." They will stay here in Anderson always, going from door to door every

Saturday morning to say, "Hi, I'm one of Jehovah's Witnesses, and I'm here to bring you some good news today." And they will pray for the people who slam the door in their faces and preach to the ones who will listen.

I press my head against the window and watch pines and oak trees move slowly by me. We will not see our mother again. The letters will be fewer and fewer until there are no more. And her voice on the phone saying "Soon, baby, soon," will come out of nowhere a year later, stay on for a few months, then slowly grow more unfamiliar. Less promising.

Charleston is not far by bus. It is bigger than Anderson and alive as New York at night. In a café, years later, I will look up and see a woman who reminds me of my mother and stand quickly, knocking my coffee over. "Ma?" I will call, and the woman will turn, look at me. And for a moment our eyes will register something—*You found me!* our eyes will say. *After all these years!* But then the light will change and the woman will become who she always was, a stranger who is not my mother. And the stranger will turn slowly, pay her check. And leave.

And somewhere inside of me, Jehovah God will settle, become a part of my blood and bones. But my fear of Armageddon and my belief in life everlasting will grow as faint as my mother's voice, as far away as the promise of her. Familiar and foreign as a stranger's face.

"Scissors, paper, rock," Scott sings.

My grandmother's back is straight.

Layana leans her head farther out the window.

Her hair is wild like Mama's.

It blows and blows and blows.

Jake slid his tray onto a table in the area he hoped was still no-man's-land. Nothing else seemed to have changed at Greenfield High School in the three years he'd been away—why should cafeteria tables?

So far he'd managed to avoid even looking at the section where he'd eaten all his school lunches three years ago. But now, without thinking, he turned his head and glanced quickly. Yep, they were still there. He'd looked too fast to recognize any faces, but he would have known those earnest expressions a mile off. The God Squad still sat by the window.

"It's more like the Goon Squad," he'd mocked them to his friends in Sulfur Springs. "And the guys in it call themselves Men of God. *I'd* call them Men of Acne. You'd think, if there really was a God, He could clear up their faces."

Somehow, Jake had always conveniently neglected to mention to his friends in Sulfur Springs that he'd once been a Man of God himself.

His friends in Sulfur Springs were cool. They tended toward leather jackets, baggy jeans, gold stud earrings. When they wore T-shirts advertising Gold's Gym, the shirts really said "Gold's," not "God's Gym," with a prickly-looking cross below and the challenge "Benchpress This." They carried condoms in their back pockets, not miniature New Testaments. They loved Jake's God Squad stories.

"Hey, tell us about the girls again," Jake's friend Marcus would urge on a slow Friday night.

"Oh, you mean the"—Jake always paused for dramatic effect—"*Pole* girls?"

"They call *themselves* that?" Marcus always asked.

"Oh, yeah," Jake always answered with a knowing grin. He'd never explained the real reason. Who cared about some nationwide movement for high school students to meet at the flagpole every morning to pray?

It was weird. Jake had never thought about the possibilities for double entendre in the Pole Girls' name until his family left Greenfield, right after his freshman year. Moving to Sulfur Springs, he'd become a whole different person. But now he was back in Greenfield.

"Can't you find some other dying Midwestern town to act important in?" he'd asked his parents when they'd announced the move. "There're dozens of them. Take your pick. I don't want to go back to Greenfield."

His mother had given him an apologetic frown.

"But your father knows the Greenfield office," she'd said. "That's why he got this promotion. He'll be in charge of the whole operation there. And won't it be nice to go back to someplace we know, instead of somewhere new again?"

Jake had heard the wistfulness in her voice and wondered briefly if she hated moving every few years just as much as he did. The God Squad Jake might have brought that up as a prayer concern at Bible study. Though he couldn't really remember, he probably had, before the move to Sulfur Springs. But the Sulfur Springs Jake couldn't worry too much about his mother's feelings.

"You mean you'd rather move somewhere you know is awful, instead of a place that has a chance of being decent?" he'd mocked her.

Jake's mom had faced him squarely, her hands on her hips.

"I thought *you* were happy there," she'd said accusingly.

"Revisionist history," he'd muttered.

Now he took a big bite of his sandwich, and made a face.

"Same imitation meat as ever," he wanted to gripe to somebody, but he was surrounded by strangers. Three years ago he'd been so into the God Squad, he hadn't really gotten to know anyone else at Greenfield High. He'd been a strange kid back then—pimples, glasses, braces. All he'd needed was a pocket protector and he'd have had his own little stereotype all wrapped up. He'd fit in with the God Squad better than he wanted to admit. But that was then. Now his braces were off, his skin had cleared up, and he'd gotten contacts. He had possibilities.

He squinted, calculating. It was November of his senior year. He was halfway through his first day back at Greenfield High, and he'd barely spoken to anyone. Was it worth trying to make friends, so he'd have someone to hang around with before he went off to college next fall? Could he even find friends like he'd had in Sulfur Springs?

"Oh! I know you!" someone said behind him.

It was a girl's voice. He turned around.

"Jake, right?" she said.

Jake looked up at the girl. She had a cloud of dark hair curling around her face, and startling green eyes. She was one of the Pole Girls, of course. No other female would possibly remember him. But when he thought of the Pole Girls, he always thought of them as a group: a horde of almost-identical, angelic-looking beauties wearing ankle-length gauze dresses and headbands. He'd never said anything about the headbands to his Sulfur Springs friends because it was too personal—three years ago, just thinking about those headbands had been enough to reduce him to a puddle of lust. It was probably psychological. There'd been so much talk in the God Squad about waiting until marriage for sexual fulfillment that he'd wanted those girls even more.

This girl wasn't wearing a headband.

"Yeah," he said. "And you're—don't tell me . . ." There was something different about her that was throwing him off. He'd known her pretty well, three years ago. She'd probably been his prayer partner once or twice. "Starts with a *K*, right? Kara, Kelly, Kayla, uh, Carob?"

"Caitlyn," she said, in a tone that made it very clear that she got the joke but wasn't going to laugh.

"Um, right. I was pretty sure your parents wouldn't have named you for fake chocolate." He gave her his best devilish grin, though it was probably wasted on a religious fanatic.

But the grin must have been worth something, because she was putting her tray down, pulling up the chair across from him.

"I heard you were moving back," she said.

"You did?" He instantly regretted the eagerness in his

voice. She was part of the God Squad. They'd probably sent her out on a reconnaissance mission. All he had to do was tell a few Antichrist jokes and she'd run away in horror, gauzy skirt tucked between her legs.

Never mind that she was wearing jeans.

"Who told you?" Jake asked, trying to sound like he didn't care.

"You know," she said, picking at her food. "There was that write-up in the paper about your dad."

"Oh," Jake said. He'd forgotten that about small towns— every time his dad shook some other official's hand, there'd be a picture of it in the paper.

Caitlyn looked him straight in the eye. "Why aren't you sitting over there?" she asked, tilting her head ever so slightly toward the God Squad tables.

Had Jake called it, or what? He decided to have a little fun. "God and I aren't exactly on speaking terms anymore," he said.

Caitlyn didn't react the way he'd expected. She kept looking at him, with such intensity he had to look away.

"Really?" she said. "Who stopped speaking first?"

So that was how it was going to be. Jake decided to take the offensive. "Why aren't *you* sitting over there?" he asked.

Caitlyn shrugged. This time she was the one to look

away. "I make them uncomfortable," she said slowly. "Ever since—well, you probably heard what happened."

Now, this could be interesting.

"No. I didn't," he said, leaning forward. He mentally flipped through the possibilities. Had Caitlyn gotten pregnant? Had an abortion? Announced she was a lesbian? Come to think of it, maybe it wouldn't be interesting. There were lots of things the God Squad wasn't comfortable with. "You forget, I've been six hundred miles away for the past three years."

"It made the national news," Caitlyn said, almost sounding irritable. "International, I mean. Newspapers, TV stations around the world—"

"I don't really follow the news," Jake said. "Not anymore." Back in the God Squad they'd been encouraged to keep up with tragedies worldwide, so they could sprinkle them into their prayers: "God, be with the seven hundred missing after the earthquake in Honduras . . . watch over the mud-slide victims in Bangladesh. . . ." For months after he moved to Sulfur Springs, he couldn't touch a newspaper or catch a snippet of TV news without feeling that sick twist of guilt in his stomach. *These people will perish without my prayers. . . .* It was all ridiculous, of course. What good did prayers do?

And what did he care, anymore, about doing good?

He pushed his attention back to Caitlyn, wondering how

her pregnancy/abortion/lesbianism/whatever could possibly have been international news.

"You'll have to fill me in," he said, feeling proud of the sarcastic spin he put on his words.

Caitlyn gave him a look that made sarcasm seem childish, like something he should have outgrown along with pacifiers and superhero underwear.

"I mean, if you want to," Jake added quickly. She wasn't bad-looking, after all. If she'd gotten kicked out of the God Squad, maybe she could be his ticket into the fun crowd in Greenfield. If there was one.

"All right," Caitlyn said. She looked past him. Jake turned around, to see what she was looking at, but there was nothing behind them but a wall. She was starting her story anyway.

"I went to Europe last summer with a high school tour group," she said in a low voice. "It was something I'd been saving for just forever. I was the only kid from Greenfield on the trip. It was supposed to be a great way to get to know kids from all over the U.S., while we were seeing the glorious sights of Europe. That's what the brochures said."

"And you believed the brochures?" Jake asked, staying sarcastic just for spite.

Caitlyn didn't seem to notice. "Yeah, I did. But they kind of . . . exaggerated. The trip wasn't nearly as well organized or well chaperoned as the brochures said. If my parents had known what it was really like, they never would have let me go." She hesitated. "By the time we got to Paris . . . well, I had a bed in a hotel room. Other than that—I was on my own."

Caitlyn explained how she had started hanging out with her three roommates at the hotel, Danielle and Kendra and Sazz. "They liked to sleep until noon, get up and shop for a while—or maybe, *maybe* walk through a museum, then go barhopping all night. They were just blown away by the idea that they could go out drinking over there, and nobody cared."

"Sounds like typical God Squad behavior," Jake couldn't help joking.

Caitlyn's laugh was bitter. "I didn't fit in at all. But I was so lonely—I didn't want them to think I was weird or anything. So I hid in the bathroom to read my Bible. I said my prayers in bed, in the dark, after the lights were out. I went to the bars with them, but I just had Coke. I said I'd always be the one who made sure we could get back to the hotel. But they still made fun of me. And I still felt guilty."

"Guilty?" Jake asked. "Why?"

"Do you know how little you get out of reading the Bible when you're scrunched up in the bathroom, yelling, 'Just a minute! Just a minute! I'll be right out'? Do you know how pathetic a prayer seems when you spend three seconds on it before falling asleep, after spending half the night in a smoky bar, dancing with drunks?" Caitlyn asked. "And I wasn't going to church. I promised my parents, when I left, that I'd go to church every Sunday. There was some line in one of the brochures about how the group leaders would find 'appropriate religious services' in each city for any teenager who wished to attend, and I think it was that line that convinced my folks it was safe to let me go. But it was just a joke to the group leaders. Everything was."

"Wait a minute," Jake interrupted. "Your *parents* are religious?"

"Yeah," Caitlyn said. "At least I used to think so. They go to church every Sunday."

"Wow," Jake said. "Mine aren't. They thought the God Squad was just some weird phase I went through. They were happier seeing me wearing a black leather jacket than a crucifix."

For the first time in three years Jake wondered if he'd just caved in to his parents' wishes when they'd moved to Sulfur Springs. If he'd found another God Squad there, would he have stayed religious? Or had he just been using the God Squad to upset his parents in the first place?

He told himself he didn't care, either way. He forced his attention back to Caitlyn. "That's expecting a lot, that you'd go to church in Europe," he said.

Caitlyn shifted in her chair. "Well, I could have. But I

didn't. Not until we toured Notre Dame one Saturday, and I saw a sign announcing a worship service in the chapel there at seven A.M. the next day. Our hotel was just nine or ten blocks away, and I thought it'd be the easiest thing in the world just to set my travel alarm, get up and go to the service, and then be back before my roommates were awake. I wasn't even going to say anything about it to them."

"So you were sneaking out to go to church," Jake said. "Kind of a reversal there, wasn't it?" He was trying to make it sound funny again, but Caitlyn didn't laugh. Her face was set in a way that reminded Jake of carved stone.

"I wasn't going to say anything," she repeated. "But, I don't know, it was like I couldn't keep my own secret. We stayed out really late Saturday night, and when we got back to the hotel, I said something like, 'It's going to be hard getting up at six thirty tomorrow,' and then everyone started asking what I was talking about. Then we got into this huge fight, because Danielle and Kendra and Sazz said they didn't want my alarm clock waking them up, or me disturbing them when I was getting dressed, and I was saying, 'I'll turn my clock off right away, I'll get dressed in the bathroom, I won't bother you.' But that just made them madder, because they said I was acting like I thought I was better than them, going to church and all. And then I said, fine, I just won't go, because I was thinking, wouldn't it be more Christian not to disturb my roommates? And I was tired anyway, and I didn't really want to go. I just thought I should, you know? So I talked myself out of it. I wasn't going to go. Do you understand? I wasn't even going to go!"

Caitlyn was almost screaming, and Jake didn't know why. A couple of the kids sitting nearby glanced over at her and then quickly looked away. Something in their expressions made Jake think that maybe they'd all heard her tell this story before, and they didn't want to hear it again. But maybe he was just imagining things.

"So you didn't go," Jake said, wondering how he could escape hearing the rest of the story.

"No," Caitlyn said. "I went, all right. I was so tired, I forgot to turn off my alarm. And then when it went off the next morning, I got up right away, and I could tell all my roommates were dead to the world"—something caught in her voice, but she went on—"and I got dressed in the dark, and none of them even moved. And then I went out, and I was still tired, and my head ached from all the smoke in the bar the night before. And it was a foggy morning, and I got lost, so I was fifteen minutes late getting to the service—I wasn't even sure I should go in. Then when I did go in, it was all in French, of course, and I don't really know French very well. I think I recognized it when they said the Lord's Prayer, but it wasn't like I could join in. And then they gave communion, but I knew I wasn't supposed to go up for it, because I'm not Catholic. . . . I didn't get a single thing out of that service. I was just going through the motions."

Now Caitlyn spoke quietly, like someone in a trance. Almost against his will, Jake leaned forward again, listening intently.

"And it was hard to hear much of the service, anyway, because there were all these sirens, the European kind, you know, that don't sound real. It was boring, and I was almost falling asleep—I was so happy when the service was over and I could get out of there. I thought I'd feel . . . better, you know? Virtuous. But I just felt foolish about the whole thing. And sleepy. I was just hoping I could go back to bed for a few more hours.

"I got lost again, walking back to the hotel. I wasn't really paying attention to anything. So, I know this sounds stupid, but I didn't notice anything until I stepped on the hose."

"The what?" Jake said.

Caitlyn just looked at him. "The fire hose," she said, as if it should have been obvious. "And everyone was yelling at me in French, but I didn't understand. Then I saw the fire trucks. And the flames. It felt like it took me a year to put it all together. The flames were coming out of the windows of my hotel. Out of the windows of the room I'd been staying in."

She spaced her words precisely. Jake wanted her to speed up. "Your roommates," he said, feeling a dread he didn't want to acknowledge. "What happened to your roommates?"

"They were dead," Caitlyn said flatly. "Everyone who stayed on the fourth floor of that hotel that night was dead. Except me."

Jake waited, but she didn't say anything else. He felt strangely disappointed. "That's it?" he said. "That's the end of the story?"

"No," she said.

But Jake was suddenly too worked up to listen anymore. "So going to church saved your life? Why did you say the God Squad isn't comfortable with you anymore? I bet they just love that story," he said. "How many sermons have you been in so far? I can just hear it: 'The sinners perished, but the girl with faith was spared from the flames.'" He laughed bitterly. "God, isn't that perfect?"

He'd had hopes for Caitlyn, but he could see now that she was only about two minutes away from asking him to join her on bended knee, to pray for repentance. She'd probably never even been to Paris. She'd probably made up the whole story. A nice little allegory to save his soul.

"Shut up!" Caitlyn hissed. "Weren't you listening? My

faith didn't save me from anything. I don't even know if I have any faith. I was just going through the motions."

Jake was stunned into silence. Caitlyn seemed to be near tears. "I can't stop thinking about this," she said. "Is going through the motions all that God requires? Is it my fault my roommates died, because I didn't invite them to church with me? Did God spare me because he has some plan for my life? Or does this mean anything at all? Just because going to church that Sunday kept me from dying, that doesn't mean I didn't deserve to die. It doesn't mean that I won't go to Hell when I do die."

Tears glittered in her eyelashes, but none rolled down her face. Jake forgot that he was supposed to be acting blasé, sarcastic, cool. "What do . . ." He hesitated. "What do your parents say? What does the God Squad say?"

"My parents say they're glad I kept my promise to go to church. The God Squad says pretty much what you said—that God saved me. But everyone says I've got to quit obsessing about it. They say I should forgive myself. They say I'm not giving myself enough credit for the depth of my faith. But I know what I'm like. I didn't deserve to be saved! I wasn't any better than the others!"

Her voice reached a high pitch, almost hysterical, and Jake knew he wasn't imagining anything this time—the kids around them were deliberately looking away, doing their best to ignore her. Back in his God Squad days he'd always wondered how people in biblical times could possibly have ignored Jesus, or John the Baptist, or any of those Old Testament prophets who went around shouting about repentance and impending doom. But now he understood. All the biblical prophets must have looked as wild-eyed and crazy as Caitlyn. Of course people crossed the street to avoid them. Of course people pretended not to see or hear. Probably every kid in the cafeteria pitied him for getting trapped listening to Caitlyn.

"What do you think?" Caitlyn practically pleaded, as if his opinion really mattered.

"I don't think you're just going through the motions anymore," Jake said.

It was a throwaway line. But Caitlyn seized on his words as if he'd said something real. "No," she said slowly. "No. You're right. I'm not."

She looked at him with such wonderment that Jake began racking his brain for a snappy putdown. Anything to divert her. Instead, his brain kept bringing up memories of his time in the God Squad—all the prayers he'd mumbled, all the Bible verses he'd read without thinking, all the sermons he'd daydreamed through. How committed could he have really been, to give it all up so easily? For the first time he wondered if his problem with the God Squad hadn't been overzealousness, but lack of zeal.

Or was his zeal just misplaced?

He didn't know. But he looked back at Caitlyn with more empathy than he'd ever thought himself capable of before.

"Hey, thanks," Caitlyn said, and almost smiled.

Suddenly Jake knew what he needed to do next. He stood up.

"Where are you going?" Caitlyn asked in surprise.

"Come on," Jake said. "Let's go make the God Squad uncomfortable together."

Kyoko Mori

The soul's journey from the earth to heaven takes forty-nine days. Kneeling in front of the Buddhist altar in her house in Kobe, Shinobu's grandmother lights an incense stick. She watches as the white smoke rises straight up, pointing the way for her son's journey. Twenty-seven days after his death he is more than halfway there. Shinobu imagines her father running up a steep mountain path full of rocks and tree roots. He is wearing the navy-blue windbreaker, the long pants, and the Adidas shoes he used to put on for his morning run. Below him white fog is rolling in. Her father stares straight ahead at the mountain peaks rising out of the clouds.

The altar, made of dark wood, has three shelves. The two lower shelves hold several cups of food and tea, a vase of flowers, the bowl for burning incense. The top shelf has a picture of Buddha and several golden tablets with the names of the family dead carved on them. Shinobu's father's name is written in black ink on a plain pine plaque. On the forty-ninth day the priest will return with a golden tablet for him—like a certificate, Shinobu thinks, a diploma that says his soul has finished its journey and joined the spirits of his ancestors.

As Grandmother bows her head in prayer, Shinobu, too, presses her palms together and closes her eyes, but she is not sure to whom she is praying. Grandmother refers to the dead people in their family as *hotoke-sama*, the Buddha spirit, or *gosenzo-sama*, the honorable ancestors. She says that the ancestors have become one with the holy Buddha and can now listen to their prayers. Every morning she asks for their blessing and protection. Two or three years ago, in middle school, Shinobu saw a film about the founders of world religions. Buddha, an Indian prince by birth, renounced his title and went to live with the poor because he had a revelation while he meditated by a lotus pond and realized that desire was the cause of human suffering. Shinobu tries to picture her Japanese ancestors seated on golden thrones with an Indian prince, but she sees, instead, a multitude of frogs perched on the round leaves of water lilies and croaking. If the ancestors have become holy spirits who can hear their prayers, what about her father, who will soon join them? With her head bowed, Shinobu wonders whether she is supposed to pray to him or for him.

At the Methodist church Shinobu attends with her mother and stepfather in Evanston, the only dead person the minister prays to is Jesus, who rose from his death to eternal life. The other dead people are sleeping in the ground until the Judgment Day, when God will call them to rise up and join the multitude of the faithful. Their memories will always be with us, the minister says when someone in the congregation dies, but we should let them go and trust their souls to God. Shinobu pictures her father sleeping in blue-and-white-striped pajamas, snoring comfortably and waiting for God. Then she again imagines him running up a mountain path toward the cloud of his ancestors. The two pictures spin in her mind and make her dizzy.

Grandmother opens her eyes. *"Ah, korede yoi,"* she says: "Yes, that's good." Shinobu nods even though she doesn't understand what is good or why. In the five years since she and her mother left Japan, Shinobu has attended Japanese classes twice a week in Chicago, but her mother, who changed her name from Reiko to Rae, doesn't speak Japanese to Shinobu at home. Shinobu has forgotten a lot. Though she has been back in Kobe for three weeks now, she doesn't understand everything Grandmother says. Even when she understands every word, the meaning as a whole feels foggy.

Shinobu picks up the tray on which her grandmother placed the cups and bowls from yesterday. Steam rises from the new tea on the altar. She follows her grandmother down the dark hallway of the old house. All the rooms, except the kitchen, are on one side or the other of this hallway: the room where the family altar is kept, the guest room where Shinobu has been staying, the room that was her father's for the last five years, and a bedroom each for her grandmother, her cousin Tomoko, and her grandfather, who spends his days on his futon.

In the kitchen at the end of the hallway, Shinobu empties and washes out the cups and bowls from the altar while Grandmother cooks Grandfather's breakfast—a thin rice gruel she will feed to him with a spoon; carrots boiled, mashed up, and put through a sieve. Since his stroke two years ago, Grandfather can chew with only one side of his mouth. His voice sounds as though he were speaking underwater.

"I'm going to call my mother," Shinobu tells her grandmother.

"What time is it there?"

"I don't know. Nighttime."

"You won't be waking her up?"

"I don't think so." *The baby wakes her up at all hours of the morning,* Shinobu thinks. She wonders if Rae told her former mother-in-law about her new son when they talked on the phone to arrange for Shinobu's visit. The baby is almost a year old now—a half brother who looks nothing like Shinobu, with his chubby pale face and light-brown hair. Shinobu hasn't mentioned him to her grandmother.

As soon as Rae picks up the phone, Shinobu can hear the baby fussing. Her mother must be in the kitchen, bouncing him on her shoulder while straightening out the counter or drying the dishes.

"Hi, it's me," Shinobu says. "Sorry I haven't called in a while."

"That's all right. I know the time difference makes it hard to call."

Outside the window of the guest room, the sun is shining on her grandparents' walled-in garden. The pine trees, trimmed a few days ago, are scarcely taller than she; each branch holds out a green clump meticulously shaped to resemble a cloud. In Evanston the tall maples in their backyard must be dropping their green helicopters of seed. Shinobu wishes she could tell her mother how much she misses the maples and her stepfather's vegetable garden, but no words come to her.

"Have you been busy?" Rae asks.

"Kind of." Every day has been the same: helping her grandmother and her cousin Tomoko with housecleaning and shopping during the day, then sitting in the kitchen at night, watching TV.

"What have you been doing?"

"Oh, just hanging out." There's another long silence before Shinobu asks, "How's the baby?"

"I'm holding him right now. He's beginning to repeat sounds. He's trying to talk." Rae used to get upset because Shinobu never called the baby by his name. "His name is Samuel," she nagged, but by now she has given up.

"So have you been to see the Gordons yet?" Rae asks.

"No, I haven't had the time."

"Did you call to find out if they're still around?"

"No, but their name's in the phone book. I looked it up." Pastor Gordon and his family live in the manse of the international church Rae and Shinobu attended when they lived in Kobe. After Rae decided to leave Shinobu's father and marry Rich, Rae and Shinobu lived with the pastor's family while they waited for their U.S. immigration papers.

"Be sure to pay them a visit."

"Okay."

Shinobu said good-bye and put down the phone. The room is empty except for a dresser and a low desk placed directly on the straw-mat floor. Her futon is folded up and put away in the closet. She closes her eyes and pictures her room with plants and candles on the windowsill, the posters on the wall, books and stuffed animals on the shelves. Shinobu was supposed to wait until college to visit her father and his family. "Going back and forth every summer will only confuse you," her mother said. "Our life is here now, with Rich. He's more like your father than your father ever was."

All the years Shinobu lived with her father, he left early for work and returned long after Shinobu and Rae had gone to bed. On weekends he ran in the morning and spent the afternoon golfing with his co-workers and clients. Shinobu couldn't blame her mother for falling in love with Rich, who was teaching in Japan for a year and attending their international church. Rae had never been like other Japanese mothers, who waited on their husbands at all hours and seldom went anywhere alone. Rae had gone to college in California; she had taught Shinobu English when she was four and sent her to an international school. Maybe she was preparing all along to marry someone like Rich and move to America. She was right about Rich being more like a father than Shinobu's father had been. Before the baby was born, he came to Shinobu's soccer meets and cheered louder than anyone else's father or mother. He was going to teach her how to play the guitar. In Evanston Shinobu had seldom thought of her father.

But when he died suddenly of a heart attack in June and Grandmother called with the news, Shinobu told Rae that she wanted to spend the rest of the summer in Kobe. She thought Rae would say, "The rest of the summer is a long time. Why not go for a week or two and come back?" Instead, Rae frowned and nodded at the same time. "That's a good idea. Your grandmother would be so happy to see you." At O'Hare Rae stepped back from their hug while Shinobu was still trying to hold on. "You're doing the right thing," she said. "I'm proud of you." Her eyes looked shiny, but she did not cry.

Down the hallway Shinobu's cousin Tomoko is sitting on the floor in front of the mirror in her room. Her head tilted to the right, she gathers her long hair over her right shoulder and brushes it, counting the strokes. "Ninety, ninety-one, ninety-two." When she reaches a hundred, she tilts her head the other way, swings her hair to her left shoulder, and starts over. The sliding door is partially open. Shinobu goes in and sits on the floor behind her cousin.

Tomoko outlines her mouth in bright red, purses her lips, and blots the lipstick on a pink tissue delicately, as though she were kissing a thin skin of air. Shinobu's father and Tomoko's mother used to be mistaken for twins until they were teenagers;

Shinobu and Tomoko have inherited their long narrow eyes, oval faces, small noses, and button mouths. Even Grandmother cannot tell them apart in their old pictures. Looking at Tomoko's face in the mirror, Shinobu can imagine her own face at twenty-one, if she were to grow out her hair and start wearing makeup.

"Are you going out?" she asks Tomoko, who is wearing a white blouse and a light-gray skirt.

"I'm going to my flower arrangement class."

Tomoko has classes every day—flower arrangement, French cooking, tea ceremony, calligraphy, piano, sewing, driving—to prepare her for her marriage. Tomoko got engaged a few months ago, but now the wedding will have to wait till next summer. It's bad luck for a family to have a wedding and a funeral in the same year. "I don't care," Tomoko told Shinobu. "I know I have to get married eventually. Now or later, it's all the same. It's only an arranged marriage." Tomoko moved into their grandparents' house three years ago and changed her last name from her father's to her mother's because her father already had two sons to carry on his family name, while on her mother's side there was nobody. Tomoko will have to marry the second son of a good family—someone who will take Grandfather's last name and save it from dying out. "I only met my fiancé twice," she said. "It makes no difference whether I marry this man or some other family's second son. Either way, it's no one I've chosen."

"Would Grandfather and Grandmother let you marry on your own if I promised to have children someday and name them for our family?" Shinobu asked. She still has her father's and grandfather's name, Fujimura, even though her mother is now Rae Brooks.

Tomoko smiled and shook her head. "It's sweet of you to say that. But no. Grandfather wants his name to go on here, in Kobe."

Tomoko turns away from the mirror and stands up. She opens her dresser drawer and takes out a tin canister, from which she shakes out a spoonful of bird food she has made. It's a mixture of suet, peanut butter, and sunflower seeds, cooked together, hardened, then chopped up. "I'm going to call Ichiguro."

Shinobu goes out to the hallway and stands behind the door, looking into the room, while Tomoko throws her window open, sprinkles the bird food on the sill, and claps her hands. Immediately there is a loud cawing and the flapping of big wings. The crow hangs in the air for a moment, wings spread open but perfectly still, before landing on the sill. Bowing his head as if to thank Tomoko, he pecks at the food. Even when he has finished eating, he stays and lets her stroke the back of his neck with her finger. He cocks his head, stretches his neck, ruffles his feathers, and will not fly away until she nudges him. Beating his strong wings, he takes off into the air, cawing loudly.

Tomoko closes the window. Shinobu imagines a nimbus of shiny black light around her cousin's hair. In the stories Shinobu heard in Sunday School, people who gave food and shelter to beggars later found out that they had been visited by angels. What you have done for the smallest of my brethren, Jesus said in the Gospels, you have done for me. Tomoko found the baby crow, who had fallen out of his nest, during the rainy season last year. She took him home, fed him, and let him fly around in her room until he was strong enough to leave. A year later he still watches for her from the rooftops and telephone poles. As soon as Tomoko goes into the back-yard or opens her window, the crow is at her side, begging for food, stretching his neck to be petted. Even from the sky he can tell her apart from other people. One afternoon Shinobu stepped outside wearing Tomoko's summer jacket. The crow cawed at her from the telephone pole. "*Kahhh, kahhh, kahhh,*" he scolded her for trying to fool him. Grandmother thinks he is a bird of ill omen, but Tomoko doesn't care. As her cousin turns away from the window and sighs, Shinobu imagines a black angel alighting from the sky to save her.

A little before lunchtime Shinobu takes the grocery list Grandmother made and walks down the hill to the supermarket near the train station. In Evanston Rich goes shopping once a week in their van, but in Kobe, no one drives to the store. The aisles are full of women with wicker baskets or string bags, buying just enough food for today. The only men in the store are the checkout clerks. Shinobu pays for the groceries and puts them in her grandmother's blue string bag.

It's almost noon, the time Tomoko's flower arrangement class gets out. The class is held in a room upstairs from a bank on the other side of the train station. The first Saturday after Shinobu arrived, Tomoko brought home the arrangement she made—white lilies and willow branches rising out of the shallow dish, looking like an intricate sculpture. The last two Saturdays, Tomoko left the arrangements in the lobby of the bank instead of carrying them home, up the steep hill of their neighborhood. Shinobu meant to go and see them but forgot. If she goes now, she may catch Tomoko just as she is leaving her lesson and placing her flowers in the lobby. The string bag has only a carton of eggs, a few vegetables, a loaf of bread. Carrying it easily in one hand, Shinobu hurries to the bank.

Upstairs, several women are packing their arrangements into boxes. Like Tomoko, they are wearing white blouses;

light-gray, brown, or blue skirts; opaque nylons, and shoes that match the skirts. Their perfume mingles with the smell of cut flowers and makes Shinobu dizzy. Tomoko is already gone. In her red T-shirt and blue jeans Shinobu feels like a foolish puppy—unruly and awkward. She bolts downstairs and runs around the building to the main entrance of the bank.

Shinobu steps onto the metal grid in front of the automatic doors. When the doors slide open, she is only three feet away from her cousin, who has just stepped onto the grid on the other side. Next to her is a tall young man in a black T-shirt and black jeans. Tomoko's hand is clasped inside his, her head leaning against his shoulder. Behind them, on the table, the irises in a white vase look like tall candles with blue flames. Her cheeks flushed red, Tomoko yanks her hand out of the young man's and covers her red mouth. For a few seconds Shinobu and Tomoko stand face-to-face across the door frame; then Shinobu spins around and takes off, sprinting down the street. She hears the doors sliding shut, but she doesn't look back. Several blocks away, when she finally stops running, the string bag bounces against her knee and almost trips her. The yellow egg yolk oozes out from the white Styrofoam carton, staining the blue strings.

"I fell down," Shinobu tells her grandmother. "I'm sorry I broke the eggs. I'll go get some more if you'd like."

"No, that's all right." Grandmother puts away the eight unbroken eggs and washes out the string bag in the kitchen sink. "Did you get hurt?"

Shinobu shakes her head.

"You should be careful." Grandmother tilts her head and frowns. Her white hair, put up in a bun, is thinning on top. Shinobu looks away from the pink skin of her scalp. "Shall we wait for Tomoko, or would you like to eat lunch now?"

"Let's not wait." Shinobu walks to the refrigerator and opens the door. "Tell me what you need. I'll help."

Tomoko comes home while Shinobu and Grandmother are sitting down in the kitchen with a bowl of noodles for lunch. She stands in the doorway, one hand on the door frame. Her face is still red, and sweat glistens on her forehead.

"Would you like to eat with us?" Grandmother asks.

Shinobu lowers her eyes and concentrates on the soup.

"No, thanks. I don't feel very well. I'll go lie down in my room."

After Tomoko disappears down the hallway, Grandmother comments on the heat, which can drain anyone's strength. "Some people like to eat cold food when it's hot," she says, "but I think quite the opposite. If you eat hot food, it draws all the heat from your body and keeps you cool." She narrows her eyes and blows on the broth, making white steam waver over her bowl.

• • •

The door of Tomoko's room is open a few inches. Except late at night when everyone's sleeping, it's rude to shut the door all the way, as though you were trying to hide from the rest of the family. Inside, the crow is hopping around on the straw-mat floor, pecking at the popcorn Tomoko has scattered for him.

As soon as Shinobu enters the room, the crow flies up onto the sill and thrusts off into the air, kicking with his black feet and beating his wings. Tomoko is seated in the corner with her back against the wall. "I'm sorry I ran away," Shinobu says as she sits down, facing her. "Your secret is safe with me."

"That was Hiroyuki," Tomoko says. "We've been friends since our first year in high school. I was going to stop seeing him when I got engaged, but now I won't be getting married for another year. He comes to meet me after my classes, and sometimes we have tea. Or we walk around the park holding hands. We've been crazy about each other for years."

"You don't have to tell me."

"But I want to. I was glad that you saw us. In a year I won't see him ever again, but you will remember us. I'll know he wasn't a figment of my imagination."

They don't speak for a long time. "Can I ask you something?" Shinobu finally says.

"Yes?"

"You already liked him when you came to this house and took Grandfather's name."

Tomoko nods.

"Why couldn't you say that you had a boyfriend and didn't want to marry someone else? Grandmother and Grandfather wouldn't make you have an arranged marriage if they knew about your boyfriend. They might be old-fashioned, but they're not tyrants."

"It isn't that simple."

"Why not?"

Tomoko shrugs. "If I didn't take Grandfather's name and have an arranged marriage, then my sister, Yumiko, would have to. She's only sixteen now."

"That's how old I am."

"I know. What's going to happen in my future can't be helped. By the time I was ten, my mother and I knew that your parents probably wouldn't have another baby, so one of us— Yumiko, me, or you—would have to take Grandfather's name and keep it from dying out. My mother said it would have to be me or Yumiko because your mother would insist that you make your own choice. Aunt Reiko was different. She didn't believe in old customs. She told my mother that she wanted you to go to college in America and not have to come back. So that left Yumiko and me. I'm older by five years. I'm not going to let my little sister have an arranged marriage while I marry my boyfriend."

Shinobu feels her throat tighten. Tomoko is in her predicament partly because her parents didn't have a son and then Shinobu and Rae went to America. She thinks of Samuel and wishes he—or another baby boy—had been born while Rae was Reiko Fujimura. "But it's so unfair," she mutters.

Tomoko shrugs. "Grandmother would say it was fate, or our ancestors' wish. I don't believe in the ancestors, but I think it might be fate."

"Maybe there is no such thing as fate, though," Shinobu suggests. "My mother always says people have free choices. When she got divorced and married Rich, she said that God would forgive her because God doesn't want us to live in misery when we can choose to be happy."

"I know she would say that," Tomoko agrees. "Even if she and you had stayed here, that's why you would never have had to be in my position. Your mother has God on her side. I don't. I don't believe in God. I believe only in fate."

Shinobu doesn't know what to say. Her cousin's fate could have been her own. It doesn't seem fair to say that she herself is protected by her mother and by God. If her grandparents had asked her to take their name and have an arranged marriage, Shinobu would have refused. She wouldn't have obeyed them in order to spare someone else. She wouldn't have acted as selflessly as her cousin has.

"I don't think fate is always bad," Tomoko explains. "Fate can sometimes help you. When Ichiguro fell off the nest, he had no choice but to lie on the sidewalk and wait. Fate was kind to him. I found him and brought him home. I had no desire to hurt him. But if someone else had found him first, they might have stepped on him, thrown him into the bushes to die, or set their dogs on him. People can be cruel."

"You don't think people are good?"

"No. I think that animals are kinder, because they only hurt each other out of necessity. If birds ruled the world the way we do now, and if a big bird found one of us hurt in a forest, I'm sure he would pick us up and take us back to his nest to take care of us. A bird would never poke at us and torture us, never cut us up to see what's inside us or feed us poison to see how long it would take us to die. If birds were in charge, the world would be a much better place." Tomoko turns back toward the window and sighs. Up in the sky somewhere her crow is flying around. From where he is, this house must look so small. Shinobu stares at the kernels of popcorn left on the floor. The unpopped seeds remind her of the Bible passage her minister reads once every few months—if you have faith the size of a mustard seed, you can tell a mountain to move and it will obey. The seeds on the floor look charred and beyond hope.

The next morning, Sunday, Shinobu wakes up at seven. Her father has been gone for exactly four weeks. He came home from his seventeen-mile run, complained about a chest pain, and sat down in the kitchen. While his mother was pouring orange juice for him, he fell forward, hitting his face on the table. By the time the ambulance arrived, he was already dead. He was only forty-five; a long-distance runner, he never smoked. His death, Tomoko would say, must have been caused by fate.

Lying on her futon, Shinobu pictures her father running. Every Sunday he rose at seven and left the house as Rae and Shinobu were getting up. He would be running his twelfth or thirteenth mile while Rae sat down next to Rich at the eight-thirty service at their church in Kobe. Under their heavy coats in winter, Rae and Rich would hold hands as they listened to Pastor Gordon's sermon. Shinobu imagines her father's fingers curled into loose fists at his sides as he ran, her mother's fingers laced with Rich's under his black wool coat.

On the day he died perhaps her father had a premonition. He might have felt unusually tired or light-headed during his run. Maybe he suspected that his soul was trying to leave his body and rise up to the sky for its forty-nine-day journey.

The night Shinobu got the news of his death, she tried to pray for him before she went to bed. She didn't know how to pray for someone who was a Buddhist. When a Jewish girl from her high school died in a car accident last year, Rae said that God is too merciful to let people go to hell just because they have a different religion. *Maybe even atheists go to heaven,* she insisted. Shinobu agreed with her then, but she is no longer sure. For all she knows, heaven is divided into different sections, like the neighborhoods in Chicago, with the people across the dividing lines regarding each other with fear and suspicion. Or people may simply disappear and become particles of dirt, as several kids in her class believe. Someday Shinobu, too, might die suddenly, and she would not know where her soul was going; as she was falling forward and her face was hitting the table, she would not know what to believe or whom to call on for salvation.

Shinobu pictures Pastor Gordon's large hands as he prayed at the table before each meal. Some nights he helped her with her math homework and said that he could see the work of God even in a mathematical theorem. Shinobu gets up and dresses. No one else is awake yet in the house. She folds and puts away her futon. In the kitchen she leaves a note on the table. "Grandmother: I went to visit some old friends. Will be back before noon." Outside, the air is already hot and sticky.

From the downtown train station, it's a short walk to the gray stone building of the international church. At the door several white-haired American ladies look at Shinobu with that puzzled expression people have when they know you but can't remember how. Shinobu smiles vaguely at them and walks upstairs to the sanctuary. The pews are occupied by young American couples and families she has never met. Except for the old ladies downstairs who have permanent jobs at colleges, the congregation has always been made up of Americans and Germans who work in Japan for a few years and then go home. Their children attend the international school Rae sent Shinobu to. Until she moved to Evanston, Shinobu had few friends she'd known for more than two years.

Shinobu accepts a bulletin from an old man at the door. He is Mr. Brady, her Sunday school teacher from the fourth grade, but he doesn't recognize her. Shinobu sits down in one of the back pews, next to a family with two American girls her age. With her eyes closed, she listens to the pipe organ and tries to pray, but no words come to her. Talking to God is no better than talking to her mother—there is so much she wants to say, but the moment she starts, her mind goes blank.

When the music stops, a woman in a black robe goes up to the pulpit and asks the congregation to rise. The only other people sitting in the front are two of the white-haired ladies. Shinobu glances at her bulletin: "Visiting Minister: the Rev. Margaret Kendall." As the organist begins to play the prelude to the hymn, Shinobu whispers to the man next to her, "Where is Pastor Gordon?"

"Pardon me?"

"Paster Gordon, the minister? Is he still the minister here?"

"Yes," the man nods. "He and his family are in the States on vacation."

Before she can say anything else, the hymn has started. It's one she has known for years.

> *This is my father's world,*
> *And to my listening ears,*
> *All creatures sing and around me rings*
> *The music of the spheres.*

At their church in Evanston they still sing this hymn, but they no longer say "our father" in their prayers. The Lord's prayer now begins with "Our parent in heaven."

"You can think of God as a mother, grandmother, or aunt

if you want to," Rae told her last year. "God is someone who cares about you. If it's more helpful to think of a different family member or even a teacher or a doctor, it's okay." Shinobu had a vision of God as a librarian then—a kindly old lady who took the books you brought back and told you that you could renew them for two more weeks even though you were late returning them.

When the hymn is over, everyone sits down. The heavy wooden doors are shut, and the church is quiet. Shinobu won't be able to leave without attracting attention. After the greetings and the announcements, one of the old women walks to the pulpit and opens the Bible.

"A reading from the Psalms," she announces. Shinobu opens the bulletin, careful not to rustle the paper. As always, there are three readings—one from the Old Testament, one from the Gospels, one from Paul's letters. Between the readings and the sermon there is another hymn. That may be her chance to slip out. She has never before attended church alone. Even if Pastor Gordon had been around, it would have been rude to tell him all her problems after not having seen him for five years. Shinobu wishes she had never come.

Up in the pulpit the woman is reading very slowly, enunciating every word, the way people do after they've taught English in Japan for too long. "'In the shadow of thy wings will

I make my refuge,'" Shinobu hears her say. *Did I really hear that?* she wonders. She starts paying attention, but by then the psalm is all about calamities and enemies, of "the reproach of him that would swallow me up." There is no more mention of wings. It's as though a bird had landed in the windowsill for a moment and then taken off again, allowing the psalmist to go on in his usual paranoid manner about traps and enemies, about being a soul among lions, surrounded by people whose teeth are spears and arrows, their tongue a sharp sword. "You don't have to like everything you read in the Bible," Rae said. "The psalms, for instance. They're not my favorite. I don't know if King David really wrote them or not. But whoever it was, that man complains too much. He sounds self-righteous and uptight."

As the reader sits down and the other old woman goes up to the pulpit to read from the New Testament, Shinobu pictures King David roaming the desert with a crazed look of thirst in his eyes, his hands and knees scratched from brambles and rocks. A huge black bird lands next to him and spreads his wings, shielding him from the hot sun. The bird is as large as a dinosaur, its supposed ancestor according to the exhibit at the Field Museum, but its down is soft and smooth. Its beak is filled with cold water for the traveler to drink. Shinobu imagines King David tipping his head back and opening his mouth like a little bird in a nest, trusting the large beak descending toward him. Tomoko may be right. If evolution had worked out differently, dinosaurs might have survived and developed into big birds that ruled the world. Perhaps they would have had civilization and religion, a concept of charity. To them humans might have been pitiful creatures who deserved mercy.

"Be merciful unto me"—that's how the psalms often begin. "Be merciful unto me." When the pipe organ begins the prelude to the next hymn, Shinobu is thinking of her mother nursing the baby, of Tomoko holding hands with her high school sweetheart, of her father running alone into his next life. *Be merciful to them*, she says under her breath. *Be merciful.* As she rises with the congregation to sing, the rustle of the clothes all around her sounds like the flapping of birds ascending to the sky.

Jennifer Armstrong

THE MARTYRDOM
OF MONICA MACALLISTER

This story started with my trip to Paris, France, the AMAZING summer of '77, although of course I didn't know at the time that THIS would come out of it, since I was so enraptured with Guy, pronounced *g-e-e, gee* as in geese as in *pâté de fois gras,* not *jee,* gee whiz, although you try having a real French boy say *"J'ai faim de tes levres"* to you, which, if you don't know, means "I hunger for your lips," try having a real French boy say THAT and not say GEE WHIZ or something real close to it.

But the thing is, aside from Guy, what really was interesting to me about Paris was these churches everywhere. REALLY OLD some of them, too, like St. Julien-le-Pauvre from the something like 1400s, and Notre Dame? Please. Very very old. And, of course, Catholic.

And people would be in these churches ON THEIR KNEES sometimes, very pious and serious, and you really can't go in without getting a very holy feeling, it's impossible not to. They're praying, they're confessing, there's incense, it's VERY dramatic. You get a holy feeling being in these old churches with the stained glass and statues and the candles and all and the ceilings just *soaring* up to heaven. I'm sorry, you just do.

And I don't know, it just seemed to me that the Catholics must be much more SPIRITUAL than the Protestants. For example, in my church, First Presbyterian, all we have for decoration is a plain cross, no Jesus on it, and it's this really ho-hum unfancy New England church with a steeple and all, but it just never felt really very holy. The Catholics have people on their knees saying prayers IN LATIN and we've got the fellowship hour with Mrs. Young's special coffee cake and then the fathers talking about getting out on the golf course.

And in the museums in Paris, I began to notice these religious paintings of people, saints and martyrs, DYING FOR THEIR FAITH. Holy Hannah! That's commitment. That's what I call really spiritual. If you can still believe in God while you're being boiled alive in oil, or HAVING YOUR BREASTS CUT OFF, well, come on. That's PASSION! I bought an art book of the martyrdoms of the saints. I spent HOURS looking at those pictures. I was so moved. Sometimes I actually could make myself cry.

I started hunting down saint paintings in the Louvre museum and in the churches, and shivers would go up my spine when I looked at them: I just *knew* I was destined for something grand. Naturally, I hoped it *wouldn't* be having my skin peeled off while I was alive, but it would be memorable. I had no doubt of it. It gave me this feeling of kinship with the saints, if you see what I mean. I think people could see this premonition of my tragic fate in my faraway eyes as I walked along the Seine.

So when I finally got home after this LEGENDARY summer in Paris, I almost could not bear my family. First, Roger—*ack*—finger down my throat. The twins, Toby and Nina, were so childish, and, okay, MiniMac was still practically a baby, but you couldn't have a decent conversation with him about LIFE. Mom was naturally busy in her studio on some idea that would probably make a TON of money like she did with the Statue of Liberty toys for the Bicentennial, which is how I could afford to go to Paris, although that's a different story. And Judge MacAllister, aka Daddy Mac, talked about nothing but his new riding lawn mower AS IF THAT COUNTS.

And the first Sunday that I'm even home, Mom said I had to go to church with the whole family.

"Your religion is shallow and meaningless," I said. "It has no blood."

Mom flipped a pancake. "Well, I am sorry you feel that way. But if you want blood, just try being late. I'll show you blood."

Roger started to laugh, but he was drinking orange juice and he snorted it up his nose by accident and let out this BELLOW that started MiniMac yelling too. Nina had syrup in her hair and was only making it worse, and Toby was playing with a Yoda action figure from the Cheerios box, Dad was reading the *Times* and on the phone setting up a golf date for after church, and I almost felt like weeping. I put my head down on the table and banged it twice. MiniMac banged his head on the table, too, until Mom slipped him a pancake shaped like a mouse head, and HONESTLY, it was all I could do not to scream. Where was the passion? Where was the drama and fire? How did I get stuck in this this this PRESBY-TERIAN family? My family was utterly devoid of spirituality. I mean, take my dad, who actually converted to Buddhism on a Rotary Exchange trip to Japan, because he wanted to see this famous moss garden in a TEMPLE of all things, but they only allowed Buddhists into the temple, so my dad said, *I'll become a Buddhist if I have to*, and so he went through this ceremony where it was all in Japanese and he finally heard the priest say

MacAllister-San, and he knew he was in. But does he actually practice Buddhism now that he's home? No. There he is out on his lawn tractor EATING A HAM SANDWICH, and I don't know a lot about Buddhism but I know they're not supposed to eat ANIMALS, DAD! So obviously, the whole conversion thing was just a CYNICAL PLOY TO SEE A BUNCH OF OLD MOSS.

Anyway, as we were driving to church in the station wagon, it came to me like a vision, like an epiphany, like a ray of light beaming into my ear—just like those old paintings of the Virgin Mary getting her surprise visit from You Know Who. We were Protestants, weren't we? Well, it was time I started protesting. I was so busy thinking about my plan that I forgot not to sing "A Mighty Fortress Is Our God."

We had a lot of stuff in our garage. Camping gear. Recreation equipment. Old croquet sets and archery sets and a badminton set with the net all tangled up so you couldn't make it straight, rusty bikes, plastic wading pools, barbecue grills, garden ornaments, you name it. The typical kind of junk that people in the SUBURBS think is FUN. There was so much stuff that it was impossible to put the cars in there. I spent a few afternoons out there that week, and then got my friend Andrew to give me a secret ride to the church on Saturday night, and then I waited for Sunday morning to see the fireworks. I was ready to see those frozen chosen white-bread Protestants howl in horror.

So when Mom said, "Time for church," I jumped into the station wagon. Naturally, I didn't let on that I was expecting anything. I am, after all, planning to be an ACTRESS. We went up the church driveway, and that was when I saw the crowd standing around the fellowship hall door. And Dad said, "What's going on there?" as he stopped to let us off before parking the car in the lot.

And Mom got this funny look on her face as she caught a glimpse of my masterpiece through the crowd and said, "If I'm not mistaken, I believe it's Saint Sebastian."

Of course, I said nothing, but I had to hand it to Mom for such a speedy I.D.: art school. I bet she'd seen a lot of paintings of old Sebastian. Anyway, I got out of the car, very nonchalant, and strolled over to the crowd to view my handiwork, and through their legs and between shoulders there it was: an old garden gnome pierced with arrows from a bow-and-arrow set that had lost most of the feathers. The gnome was tied to a croquet stake with rope and had red-paint blood dripping down from the arrow wounds. I could hear the crowd murmuring as I approached. Mentally, I prepared myself.

"That is the funniest thing I ever saw," Mrs. Thatell said. "I hate those gnomes. It's about time somebody murdered one."

Mr. Keeler guffawed. "I bet the garden center could make a fortune if it sold 'em like this."

I stopped in my tracks. My blood actually RAN COLD and I'm not sure but I think I turned pale. They didn't get it. How could they actually NOT GET IT? Didn't they see it for what it was? A scathing indictment of their own shallow, passionless, unquestioning churchgoing routine? The gnome wasn't the point, man! It was the martyrdom. I almost went over and kicked that gnome right in the arrows, and believe me, it was all I could do to sit through the church announcements about how Mrs. Reeves had a broken hip and could people please volunteer to make suppers for her, and how the junior choir would not have practice that week because Mrs. Alice Jordan, the church organist and choir director, was going on a retreat for church organists and choir directors, and there was absolutely no red-faced indignant outcry about the monstrosity of desecration out by the fellowship hall door or what it could be saying about them all and I THOUGHT I WOULD EXPLODE IN A BALL OF FIERY FLAMES!

My family had a lot to say about it on the way home from church, though—just try getting them to shut up about anything—except that *Mom* didn't say a word. I wasn't sure if she sent me the evil eye as she was buckling the twins into their seat belts, but I acted as though I hadn't a care in the world.

Inwardly, though, I was planning my next move.

The people in my church were obviously such spiritual zombies that they didn't know an insult when they saw one. The fact that they didn't even object to it made me even more determined to shake them up. How about a little OUTRAGE, people? How about STICKING UP FOR GOD? Didn't they even have the spirit to be a little upset, for Pete's sake?

That night I made sure my door was locked before I got my book of saint paintings out from the bottom of my sock drawer. I turned the pages carefully, to avoid the slightest rustle as I looked for another good martyrdom. St. Sebastian had been a gift, really. An easy one. It didn't take someone with a Ph.D. in fine art and art history like my mom to I.D. *him*. Others would be harder.

There was St. Agnes, who was burned, even though the flames did not consume her, and then she was beheaded. I thought I could probably get the head off a gnome, but would people understand who it was supposed to be? St. Catherine was beheaded too, and milk flowed from her gaping neck. Maybe I could do something with plaster of Paris, make a fake stream of milk. The problem of course was that Protestants don't believe in saints, so the identification might be tricky on these. Of course, I could always make labels.

At last I settled on Saints Darius and Chrysanthus, two

guys who were stoned to death in a sandpit because of their faith. I got my friend Andrew to help out again when it came to the setup, which took a lot longer that Saturday night, and believe me, I was glad the minister's family was big on Saturday-night bowling with the youth group TO WHICH I DID NOT BELONG, so they weren't there in the manse next door to the church. Andrew was very uncurious about my project. He has no religion at all, just camping and guitar, and when I tried to explain what I was doing, he just said, "Cool." St. Sebastian was still there, believe it or not, nobody even CARED ENOUGH to remove him, so we set up a few feet closer to the fellowship hall door.

Sunday morning I practically flew downstairs for breakfast, and when MiniMac spilled grape juice on his clothes and Mom had to take him upstairs to change, I started tapping my feet under the kitchen table, trying not to look anxious, but inside I was thinking HURRY HURRY HURRY WE'LL BE LATE FOR CHURCH!

It was a beautiful morning. Being fall and everything, the leaves were turning colors, and the sky was very bright blue, like Virgin Mary–robe blue. From the corner of my eye I glanced over to the fellowship hall door as we pulled up the driveway, and sure enough, there were gobs of people standing around. This time I knew there would have to be some sparks flying. Fortunately, I didn't have to make myself walk slowly, because the twins and MiniMac wanted to see what everyone was looking at, and they jumped out of the car and ran, so I ran after them—and I could see our minister, Mr. Young, standing in the group. My heart beat faster. I felt like the Roman Christian martyrs going into the Colosseum to meet the ravenous lions.

Mrs. Larissa Clark was reading the sign out loud. "'Saint Darius and Saint Chrysanthus.' Interesting. Why are they wrestling in a sandbox? Is that a Catholic thing?"

Mr. Young had his hands in his jeans pockets—he was one of those new-style ministers who wear casual clothes under their robe, and he didn't have his robe on yet. He shook his head. "I don't think they're wrestling, Larissa. Maybe somebody knocked them over. Here." And he REACHED DOWN AND STOOD THE GNOMES UPRIGHT!

I shouldered my way to the front of the crowd. My head was REELING with disbelief. Blood-splattered (well, red-paint-splattered) gnomes lying among a bunch of rocks in a sand-filled wading pool and someone thinks they're WRESTLING?

"Is the sand supposed to be the Holy Land?" asked someone whose name I didn't know.

I couldn't bear it. I walked away. I now knew what the

phrase *gnashing your teeth* means, because believe me, I WAS GNASHING MINE!

I went into high gear that week, laying my plans. I was inspired by this incredible ZEAL, as though I was ready to go to any lengths to make my point. They needed it spelled out for them—FINE, I would spell it out. We'd see how they liked St. Lawrence.

Next Sunday we were walking from the church parking lot, and really, I think the whole congregation was standing outside the fellowship hall, looking at my latest creation. There was St. Lawrence, being roasted alive on a grill, and the label recorded his noble words: "Turn me over, I'm done on this side."

"Who's got the barbecue tongs?" Mr. Washburn asked.

"I like my saints medium rare," added Barry Herzog.

I didn't even stick around to hear the rest. I don't think I heard a single thing during the church service that morning. When it was over, I followed silently behind the crowd into the fellowship hall, where as usual people were having coffee and cake and talking about the school play and what their kids were dressing up as for Halloween and whether they were going to visit relatives for Thanksgiving and how many more weeks of golf there might be and offering to lend power tools or asking about each other's health and the little kids were all running around between the grown-ups' legs and snatching too many pieces of coffee cake off the table. The members of the church youth group were helping serve coffee and bringing cups to the old people who sat in the chairs along the wall. Chit chat chit chat. Where was God in all this socializing, I ask you? I wished a bolt of lightning would strike me down where I stood, just to see if anyone noticed.

And just to TWIST THE KNIFE IN MY HEART, people were also talking and laughing about the gnomes, saying how cute and funny it was, what a wacky practical joke, your typical teenage prank, those nutty kids what will they think of next, maybe it was some kind of pre-Halloween joke. They all wanted to know who was doing it, of course. I suspected that once they actually had a culprit, there would finally be some anger. There was a ringing in my ears. I would welcome their anger. I wanted to see them UP IN ARMS, DEFENDING THEIR FAITH! I WANTED TO SEE THE WRATH OF GOD!

"I know who desecrated the church!"

The fellowship hall went silent. Mom and Dad sort of maneuvered themselves to the front, and so did Mr. Young, the minister. Everyone was looking at me, arrows and stones of disapproval and outrage hurtling my way. Or so I thought.

Mr. Young cleared his throat. "Monica, do you mean you know who set up those gnomes?"

I raised my chin. *Bring on the boiling oil and red-hot pincers. Bring on the ravenous beasts.* "YES!"

Mom was beginning to get that *oh-jeez* look. Everyone was staring at me, moving just a little bit closer, a mob ready to strike. I flung my arms wide. "It was me!"

I squeezed my eyes shut and tipped my face toward Heaven. I was ready for whatever they wanted to throw at me—burning arrows, flaying, being grounded. A few seconds ticked by. No one said anything. I opened one eye. This was *very odd*.

Mr. Young was shaking his head and smiling. "Well, I must say, Monica," the minister began. "It's very creative. I love it."

"You have your mother's artistic nature," Mrs. Young added. Then she winked. "Better not let the folks over at Saint Gregory's see your handiwork, though."

People smiled and sort of chuckled, and then all at once, it seemed, the crowd went back to talking about the Wilsons' new baby that was coming all the way from Korea, and how sad it was that the Kanes had that fire and how about starting a clothing collection for them, and I saw Dad holding MiniMac on his hip as he shared a joke with Mr. Van Tassel, and Mom was shouting to deaf old Mrs. Winner, who was nodding and smiling and patting her knee—and I stood there in the center of the church fellowship hall among all my generous neighbors with my arms still flung wide, until someone put a piece of Mrs. Baxter's special coffee cake in my right hand and a cup of warm cider in my left hand.

They tasted pretty good.

Joyce Carol Thomas

HANDLING SNAKES

And these signs shall follow them that believe;
In my name shall they cast out devils;
they shall speak with new tongues;
they shall take up serpents;
and if they drink any deadly thing, it shall not hurt them;
they shall lay hands on the sick, and they shall recover.

                              Mark 16:17–18

Letitia scrunched down in her seat and eyed the wooden cage near the pipes under the organ. The cage was positioned so the organ music could sweep through the cage's cedar slats and work its lulling charm.

"I say it is better to light one candle!" said the preacher at the pulpit, thumbs hooked in his vest, declaring his text.

". . . Than to curse the darkness!" echoed the deacons, who, acknowledging the title of this Sunday's sermon, turned in white-gloved unison and marched back to their appointed places at the ends of the aisles.

During the morning service at the Church by the Side of the Road, the congregation testified and prayed, thanking God for His plenty, for the women had cooked Sunday supper already, a bountiful meal of stewed rabbit, or fried catfish and corn bread, and lemon pound cakes and berry pies and vanilla ice cream left cooling on shady porches in ice-packed churns.

Little Letitia Jones, sitting in the front row with her grandmother, was thankful for the candied country yams and tender turnip greens awaiting her and that this Sunday they were not hosting the minister, so she could eat all the chicken her appetite relished and wouldn't have to share the crunchy drumsticks with the preacher or mind her manners about piling her plate too high with creamy potato salad and feathery-light rolls.

Warmed up and getting deeper into his text, the preacher clutched his Bible close to his shiny black lapel and, reaching the climax of his sermon, declared, "It is better to light one candle than to curse the darkness!"

There would be plenty of candles lit tonight, thought Little

Letitia. And maybe tonight she would finally get rid of the Little part of her name and just be plain old Letitia. She was, after all, now twelve years old and two days, going on thirteen. A birthday to remember—not only for her grandmother's stack cake layered sweet with dried apples, red rhubarb, and plump strawberries and topped with twelve twinkling candles—but also because she was finally at last twelve, going on thirteen.

The preacher's sermon slowed down, then raced to its conclusion. The music woke up and stirred an old-timey hymn. The snaggle-toothed keys on the piano, the twanging strings on the guitar, and the dusty pipes on the pumping organ commenced blending together as Letitia's Grandmother Jones cried her usual praying tears for Letitia's mother and father, gone to the big city to make their living.

"Better to light one candle!" the preacher thundered between verses of the hymn. And every time he added that admonition, somebody would go tearing down the aisle like a candle on fire.

An outside observer would have thought the high point of the service had been reached, but Letitia knew better. They hadn't even started the snake handling yet.

"Why do they handle snakes?" she had asked her grandmother that morning at the breakfast table, as she leaned her elbows on the red-and-white checkered tablecloth over a platter of hot buttered grits, farm-fresh scrambled eggs, and Grandma's special turkey sausage.

"To test the power of God," Grandma Jones answered, wiping a fat biscuit with sweet muscadine jelly.

"But sometimes they get bit," said Little Letitia.

"Uh-huh. Hit's the truth," said her grandmother softly. And that's all she would say. It was a mystery to Letitia, this snake handling and testing the power of God.

At the Church by the Side of the Road, Letitia squirmed in her front-row pew just thinking about it. Sure as her name was Letitia, it wasn't over till the snakes.

Her grandmother stopped fanning with the mortuary fan, shot Letitia a look, and whispered, "Honey, you like a worm in hot ashes. Quit fidgeting!" Letitia tried to stay still. But nobody else was still. They danced, springing all over the aisles and up and down the benches.

Then Deacon Powers walked over by the organ, reached down and opened the cedar slat door, and took the snake out of the wooden cage. The snake had been caught high up in the mountains. That's where the biggest rattlers nested. And the thickness of mountain-red dust still clinging to the reptile's skin made Letitia know they had hiked way up past the hills and to the topmost mountain in the county.

Somebody must have been visiting the stills, Letitia

figured. When somebody did or said something crazy, her grandma would say, "They musta been visiting the stills," talking about the secret stills where the moonshine was brewed strong. Liquid courage in a mason jar, thought Letitia.

Whoever had caught this rattler, either Deacon Powers or one of his friends, must have been visiting the stills for sure before they went after this one. She was used to seeing good-sized snakes, but this one looked like somebody's prizewinner who'd been around a long, long time and had probably seen more than one deacon step back and leave him alone and reach over and grab a more medium-sized specimen.

This was a many-foot-long rattler boasting the bluntest tail Letitia had ever seen.

With the greatest care Deacon Powers gingerly laid the sleepy snake across his shoulders. And the diamond-studded rattler, who had at first seemed to be in a stupor, came to life and slid around the deacon's neck like a gigantic necklace and turned his head outward as though scanning the audience.

The rattler's jelly eyes set on Little Letitia. "Look what they got me up here doing," the snake seemed to say. "Why, I'd rather be out crawling in the weeds and sunning on the rocks than stuck up here 'round this deacon's wrinkled neck."

Letitia shivered.

A sudden chill went down her spine and shook her entire

body when she figured she could understand the snake's thoughts.

She scooted farther down in her seat, but the snake's eyes stayed unblinkingly lit on her, lit like a candle that would never go out.

It was customary for the snake to be handed down the row from one person to the next. Always before, they had left Letitia out. You had to be twelve years old before you could handle snakes.

Deacon Powers, wanting to pass the snake to Letitia and wanting to be the first to let Letitia take part in the ceremony, raised his right arm to grasp the snake behind the head. Catching the deacon's sudden movement, the snake wriggled, rattled dryly, then struck like lightning, fangs slicing down through the deacon's hairy skin and on down into the flesh of that right arm.

In no time at all the deacon's arm turned blue, swoll up, and cracked. It looked like somebody had taken a red-hot razor and pulled straight down and cut through blue skin, gray tissue, and throbbing blood.

"My God, my God!" screamed the deacon. He rolled to the floor and cried out one wrenching, awful wail of agony. But he didn't roll for long.

And Little Letitia, sitting on the front row, couldn't move.

She just knew the snake would get her next.

The snake slid away from the deacon, looked around, looked back at Letitia, then started to shake his rattles.

Grandma Jones sat up straighter in her seat and laid her fan in her lap. Something seemed to coil inside her, she was so still. Then, all of a sudden, the snake changed his mind when he spied a hole in the random-planked wood floor.

Much to Letitia's relief the snake was soon gone, the hollering was gone, and so was Deacon Powers.

It didn't surprise Letitia one whit to hear the preacher complain, "In order to test the power of God I say you got to have a clean heart. The deacon's heart wasn't clean enough for the Lord."

"Poor, poor Deacon Powers," Letitia said under her breath. Little Letitia knew the tragedy wouldn't keep the members of the Church by the Side of the Road from holy-rolling in the grass at the cemetery and romping across the stick and marble tombstones. In fact, in the name of grief it was an opportunity they wouldn't miss.

And so it didn't surprise her either to look up at the podium and hear the preacher announce, "Little Letitia Jones has reached the age of reason. Being twelve year old, she is now responsible for her own sins. This evening we will gather at the river for her baptism."

And the dead deacon not cold yet on the floor in front of the altar.

As she walked home with her grandmother, one part of her mind was on the lookout for snakes; she bravely kicked the rocks and clutched her Bible and repeated, "It is better to light one candle than to curse the darkness." Somewhere between mourning for Deacon Powers and looking forward to Sunday supper and looking for snakes, she thought of the candles the church members would light for the baptism service at the river, and reached in her pocket for her harmonica. While her grandmother hummed, Letitia mouthed the harp all the way home, playing "Shall We Gather at the River?"

In the myrtle-thick back garden squatted the big black iron pot, burned smutty by years of wood fires set under it. Letitia's grandmother's grandmother had used it for boiling clothes. It sat in its own space in a clearing that danced with lobelia and betany, surrounded by spurge and pipsissewa plants—herbs used by the Choctaw for curing colds and fevers; near it too grew the bushy sassafras tree, and lovely snapdragons and fire flowers and snakeberries that looked as innocent as miniature strawberries.

Letitia reached up into the limb of the hickory tree growing in the center of the circle near the pot, swung down a long wooden spoon, and fished the clean ball of cotton cloth out of the black iron pot her grandmother had boiled it in since first thing in the morning, shook out the sheet, and hung it on a hickory limb for the sun to bleach dry.

It would lie folded and waiting. Her heart would be clean enough, she hoped, as clean as this white sheet she'd wear at the river.

Sun down. Moon up. And the people marched to the river, their candles and the moonbeams making the silver leaves of the weeping willow trees tremble lower over the water.

First the county drunk, sobered up from moonshine, waded into the river to be baptized.

"I baptize you in the name of the father, in the name of the son . . ."

And the county drunk sank down into the water and came up speaking in tongues. The folks joined in, proclaiming, "Hallelujah!" while the county drunk kicked and shouted about "I'll go and sin no more!" and in general made a joyful noise at the top of his lungs.

Next the drunk's wife pushed her way forward to be baptized. She started crying and calling on the Lord even before she reached the preacher. About her, Letitia's grandmother had warned, "Don't ever tell that woman your business. She got more mouth than a goat got horns!"

The county gossiper was so big that Letitia just knew there'd be trouble. And there was. When the mountain of a woman sloshed down into the water, she dragged the preacher down with her, holding on to him for dear life. And so it was that the preacher got baptized again along with the county gossiper in Stinking River.

Now Little Letitia remembered why they called the river Stinking River. It was where, when the hottest days of summer came, the smell of fish, the sweaty smell of moonshine-drinking young folk, and the smell of toad frogs and ripe mud mingled to create a stink that reeked for miles around.

And the sharp smell of snakes dominated all other aromas. She'd heard somebody once say that Stinking River was where the snakes held their annual convention.

She remembered Theotis Brown last summer diving into Stinking River for a swim and coming up with twelve water moccasins stuck to his head, like they were sucking his brains out. He didn't last one minute, the poison so close to the brain, the snakes holding on.

"Letitia Anne Jones!"

She hadn't heard the preacher the first time, she was in such deep thought.

"Letitia Anne Jones!"

And now the preacher was calling Letitia Anne's name

the third time, and she was standing ready in her boiled, bleached sheet. Her grandmother's grip held so strong, Letitia had to wrench her hand free and walk through the crowd of people and up to the preacher like a grown-up.

She stepped bare feet into the bone-chilling stream.

"I baptize you in the name of the . . . holy ghost!"

And Little Letitia went down in the cold water dressed in the clean white sheet, and Letitia Jones came up hollering in the muddy white sheet, splotched with stains and river debris, her arms flailing.

Everybody started moving when they thought they heard her shout, "God's been good, for goodness' sake!"

The louder she hollered, the louder their joyful cries to the Lord, just about drowning her out. With arms outstretched up toward Heaven, they ran under the weeping willow tree limbs like they were running benches in church.

Letitia's grandmother dodged her way through the crowd of writhing people, heading for her jumping granddaughter, as the preacher proclaimed, "The young lady's got a clean heart. God's been good, for goodness' sake!"

And the people went into another frenzy of skipping and flipping in the mud banking the river, in the weeds, through the pipsissewa, fearless of snakes.

And Letitia's grandmother was bearing down on the

crowd, moving folks out of her way like they were sticks.

At last Letitia's grandmother reached the deacons responsible for keeping her granddaughter from dancing in the spirit so hard she hurt herself.

"Turn her loose!" hollered Grandma Jones. Then the grandmother yanked harder when she heard what her grand-daughter was really saying.

"God, I been bit by a snake!"

At last she succeeded in pulling Letitia away from the overcome deacons, so intent on holding on to somebody just touched by the power of God. As if they believed that they benefited by being in her very presence, they didn't want to let her go.

"Whew!" said Grandma Jones after Letitia was free. Grandma Jones decided, looking closely at Letitia's bleeding foot once she was a little bit away from the deacons, "No snake. You just stepped on one of them busted moonshine jars."

After Letitia hobbled to a clearing of grass, Grandma Jones measured her granddaughter's pulse with her fingers and calculated the flow of blood jetting out; quickly she tore off part of the wet muddy sheet and with her palsied hand wrapped it tight around the wound and applied pressure.

"No snake," she said, looking closely. "Young moonshine-drinking fool kids and their sharp pieces of glass. Humph!

"You got a clean heart, Letitia," she added as the bleeding ebbed. "Always did."

"I thought I'd tested the power of God and come up wanting," said Letitia as she studied her grandma's expression.

As the leaves and twigs danced around them, the grandmother just shook her head.

"How'd you know I was hurt when nobody else did?"

"I ain't been in this world all these many years for nothing. I was looking at your face. While your feet looked like they was getting happy, your face wasn't. And anyhow your voice sounded too growed-up, like a snake took all the gladness out of it."

After listening to that sage wisdom, Letitia paid close attention to her grandmother's next words. Her grandmother knew all about these things. If Letitia could picture God, God would look just like her grandmother, loving, kind, and a good cook.

"Letitia, I tell you the truth, sometimes the power be needing a little help," said the grandmother. "The clean sheet did it. So clean I say it could scare away a snake and stop up the blood. I ought to know—I boiled it myself!"

And Letitia was looking at the mud on the splotchy sheet. And although she knew her grandma's eyesight was failing, she could not help but notice the gleam in her glance, bright enough to put to shame the glow of twelve quaking candles.

And then she listened for the silence between her grandmother's words. What wasn't said was just as important as what was. Moreover, she decided, what her grandma saw and what she said didn't necessarily have to match. Or sometimes, when it came to Letitia, it had to match exactly. *Maybe*, thought Letitia, *there's a larger message here*. If she hadn't learned anything else, she had glimpsed at least the first riddle in handling snakes.

M. E. Kerr

GRACE

Sunday mornings when my father stepped up to the pulpit, I could almost hear the congregation groaning inside, saying to themselves: *Here we go again, another of Yawn's boring sermons.*

The best thing about Reverend Edward Yourn was that he looked so earnest and impassioned. Sincere blue eyes, silky black hair, this fine smile—I hoped I'd keep looking like him, because he's great that way. If you hadn't heard him begin by announcing that his subject that morning was "Worship as a Time for Realignment," you might have thought he was going to kick off a really provocative meditation the way they say Father Garzarella does at Holy Family. The sermon board down there promised things like "I Don't Believe the Bible," and "Heeeeerrrrre's Jesus!"

Dad's announced "Religion Without Righteousness," or "The Meaning of Redemption."

"Daddy has a more formal style," my mother claimed. "Some people prefer that."

"Mom, his nickname is Yawn. In college they called him Snore."

"It's just a play on our last name, Teddy."

"I don't have nicknames like that. And I'm Ted, or Teddy Yourn. Dad is always Edward."

"Not always." Mom smiled. "I call him lots of things besides Edward."

I am not a religious person. Dad said that a good many Preacher's Kids, in their teens, were not religious people. P.K.s have to grow into it, Dad said.

I was fifteen. "I don't think I ever will," I told him. "You *always* were. We're different."

"How do you know I always was?"

"The kids called you Preacher in your high school yearbook."

He'd get red whenever I mentioned the yearbook. He was probably afraid I was going to tease him about the infamous inscription from Taylor Train, known to us rock fans as Choo Choo or Chooch.

Dad went to school with him back in Columbia, Missouri.

When Chooch played concerts out in Montauk, about five miles from us on Long Island, the tickets were sold out months ahead of time. Locals would give up trying to get tickets, there were so many presolds, so many scalpers in on the action. And he literally stopped traffic. It was a good time to head for the beach.

When I was younger and stupid, I'd bring out Dad's yearbook to show kids. Who'd believe Dad not only went to school with Choo Choo but also was on the same page with him? That was before I knew that what I was really showing everyone was that my dad was a dork, world-class. The kids in his class wrote stuff like "Best wishes to The Preacher from Paul," or "Good luck, Edward, with your ambition to spread the good word! Marilyn!"

The only one who wrote anything beyond one polite sentence was Taylor Train. He drew a bubble over his own head with zzzzzs inside it, and made his eyelids look closed. Then he drew an arrow over to Dad's photograph and wrote *This is me listening to you preach someday in the future, Edward! I bet you convert the world to atheism! Why is it always losers who go after sinners? T. T. Train.*

"No one's asking you to be religious," Dad said. "Just have grace."

"Grace under pressure." I smirked, regretting it instantly, because I really wasn't out to get Dad. I loved him. But he'd put that Hemingway quote about grace up on the sermon board once, and someone had taken a magic marker and drawn underneath it this picture of a naked girl being stomped on by a grinning gorilla.

"Don't ever let any joker spoil the word *grace* for you, Teddy," Dad said. "I don't ask you to believe in anything you can't yet feel, but I do hope you'll have grace."

"That sounds a little dirty to me, Dad." Why was I always after him? Was it because he embarrassed me Sundays with those zzzzz sermons? Was I just self-conscious being a non-believing P.K.?

Dad said, "When you learn what grace is, it won't sound that way to you."

"I know what it is. It's doing the right thing."

Dad said, "It's doing the right thing and then more."

We left it at that.

When I was a little kid, I idolized Dad. I thought he was the best, and all I wanted to do was grow up and be like him.

Then little by little—a little more every year—it began to dawn on me that he wasn't this great knight in armor I'd made him out to be. He was far from it.

Even people in his own congregation thought he lacked charisma. Some of the younger members said the day would come when the old diehards would pass away. Then they'd junk Dad.

The way I learned about all this was the way kids in a small town hear the word about their parents: "My father says your father is . . ."

Not up-to-date. Not bringing in enough young people because he's behind the times. And the old familiar word: *boring*.

I remember a Sunday when we had a covered-dish dinner after church at the manse. It was over in a few hours. Meanwhile, Holy Family got bused down to the beach to dance and picnic, staying to watch the sunset. Even First Methodist thought up the idea of a sleigh ride one winter, going from house to house to pick up the parishioners and take them to the church hall for a square dance. Rabbi Silver, a big movie fan, instituted Flick Night on the synagogue grounds, Thursdays.

You couldn't fault Dad when it came to helping families get through illnesses or hard financial times—he was always right there in a pinch, but folks said he was better at sympathizing than socializing.

Mom was a little that way herself. She was better at repairing broken dolls and dressing them up for the Christmas boxes, and baking things for our churchyard Books and Cookies sales . . . but her idea of a Saturday night was reading a book, while Dad (always a last-minute writer) worked on his sermon. Sometimes the three of us watched an old film, or played Scrabble.

In church I went through the motions, and I suffered through the sermons. (*Good Lord, Dad, don't tempt Fate with a sermon on "How We Silence the Bible." You raise the question "But How Do We Silence the Minister?"*) I became an okay athlete (soccer, tennis, wrestling), and I was in all the school plays. I grew to look like Dad, so I was fairly popular.

Then in my senior year I fell in love with a Korean girl named Jenifer Koh.

Because of her, that last year of high school was perfect. Both of us had jobs at the Gap after school. Both of us thought about skipping college, going right to New York, where I'd try out for theater and Jenifer would get a job in fashion. Both of us were into the same things: same music, same books and movies, same way of hanging out. We just plain enjoyed each other.

The only thing we didn't agree on was the postgraduation dinner party at Springside Inn. I wanted to skip it. We were going to the prom two weeks before the ceremony, and that was enough celebration from my point of view. But Jenny said she'd feel let down if we didn't have someplace to go after we were in our caps and gowns, particularly if the other seniors had plans.

Not all the other seniors *did* have plans. The party at Springside was going to cost a lot. A special jitney would take us up there, and a photographer would be tailing us to make sure we'd have a permanent record of the evening. Long Island T was playing for dancing afterward. It would come to $300 a couple.

Dad wanted me to take our names off the list.

"You don't have to pay for it," I said. "I have savings." He was already shelling out for the prom.

"That isn't why I don't want you to go, Ted. I've heard that some of your classmates feel left out. It's one thing to splurge for your high school prom—okay—but it's something else when right on top of it there's this special party for the elite after the graduation ceremony. I don't like it."

"What does that mean, that I can't go?"

"It means I wish you'd reconsider."

"Jenny really wants to do it, Dad. All our crowd is going!"

"Maybe when I tell her what *I* have planned, she'll change her mind."

"Oh, Dad." I couldn't imagine what he thought he could come up with that would make anyone change their minds, much less Jenifer.

"Well, Teddy, I've made some calls and word is out. I'm opening the Meeting House hall for a party after the ceremony. Fortunately, people can just walk here from school."

I groaned again. "Dad, no one wants to come to the First Presbyterian Meeting House to celebrate!"

"Free of charge."

"Dad, you couldn't *pay* kids to do it!"

"I think you're wrong about that, Son."

"Don't do this to yourself, Dad."

"It's already done. Taylor is coming by about eight o'clock. Everyone will have eaten by then. We'll have our ladies prepare their roast chicken and mashed with—"

"Wait a minute. . . . Wait. Taylor?"

"I think you call him Chooch."

"Choo Choo Taylor is coming here?"

"He has a concert the very next night in Montauk. He said he thought it would be fun."

Mom piped up. "He said, 'Hey, Preacher Man, that sounds like it'd be a ball!' I was on the extension."

Mom was all smiles, her face aglow, and Dad looked pretty pleased with himself. He said, "We're not going to tell the newspapers ahead of time."

"We know all the names of the kids who aren't on the Springside list, and we're quietly calling them," Mom said.

"Are you telling them Chooch is going to show up?"

"Of course," said Mom. "We're asking them to try and keep it to themselves. We just don't want gate-crashers."

I kept looking from one to the other, unable to believe my ears. "Dad, did you just call him up out of the blue? Did he remember you?"

"Oh, he remembered your father, honey. We told the concert manager that Reverend Yourn had to get in touch with Chooch, and before we knew it, he called back. He said, 'How long has it been, Edward?' I was on the extension!"

"I can't believe you had the nerve!" I told Dad.

"He had the nerve," Mom said, "because he wasn't doing it for himself."

"Oh, I'll be glad to see Taylor again," said Dad.

Jenifer couldn't believe it, either. I'd never even told her about Dad going to school with him, because I didn't want to drag out the yearbook to prove it . . . and then have her see the zzzzzz's.

Jenifer liked Dad. She said he was a little like her own father: reserved.

"My grandfather was a preacher too," I told her. "He was reserved too."

"Of course we're going to cancel Springside," Jenifer said.

"Choo Choo Train!" Jenifer said. . . . Jenifer said, "I can't believe it, Teddy!"

In school those last weeks I'd suddenly see a sly grin on the face of little Buddy Tonsetter, whose backpack always seemed bigger than he was, or a wink from Ellie Tutton, who was a foster child in this big family that specialized in kids of all colors and races. I felt a nudge in the hall from Karl Renner, whose dad had died of heart failure at Easter; and Dana Klaich, who worked at the Gap with Jenny and me, gave me a two-fingered salute in cafeteria.

There were some cynical looks, too, from the wiseacres who hung out and mocked every tradition, ceremony, holiday—whatever; they were above it. Cal, Peter, Leary, Judge. But they weren't above Chooch. One of them would call out something like "We'll be seeing you, Yourn," in this singsong threatening way, as though they were saying: Your old man better produce, kiddo!

I was getting nervous, then more nervous, then terrified.

Holy Cow, I thought, *this is going to be some big mess if Chooch doesn't show . . . and why should he show? He didn't even like my father. Why should he show?*

That was like a chant in my head: *Whyshouldheshow? Whyshouldheshow?* The night before graduation I actually prayed. I don't pray often, because I don't think there's anyone really there to hear me, but *I* could hear me, and it was reassuring to me that I'd go to any lengths not to have this turn out the way I was ninety percent sure it would.

All through graduation that was what I thought about. At least someday I'd be able to tell my kids what was on my mind back then. How many parents can claim to remember that?

I prayed: *Please let him come. Please don't let this be a disaster.* I thought: *Is this praying or thinking?* I thought: *Is this wishing or dreading?*

I thought: *Oh shut up, Teddy! What will be will be!*

And then . . . then there we all were in the Meeting House, seated at four round tables decorated with roses from our garden, a few white balloons floating overhead . . . and Mom had even gone through my CDs to find Chooch's music. It was right up front with Mick Jagger, Billy Joel—all the ones who'd been around forever and would last that long, too. They were the ones at the heart of rock 'n' roll, the kind of performers who could make kids go ape.

Chooch's voice was rocking through the speakers.

The church ladies had cooked up a storm, and everybody was scarfing it down, talking, laughing, having a good time. But everybody was looking toward the door, too—in high gear, waiting, watching the clock.

Then it began. "Choo Choo Choo Choo"—kids imitating a train the way they did at his concerts when he'd walk onstage with his guitar strapped to him. "Choochoochoochoochoo!"

He had come in the back way.

He was slapping the backs of the boys at the first table, and blowing kisses at the girls, and they had started the *choo*-ing. Now the whole place was making that noise, and kids were on their feet, clapping, with Chooch heading toward my father's table, where there was a mike.

My father stood up, and Chooch gave him a sock on the shoulder, then leaned down and shook hands with my mother. "Shut up now!" he said over the mike. "I'm going to sing for my supper. I'm going to sing two songs now and then I'm going to eat. Then I'm going to sing two songs more, and I'm out of here!"

He sang his big hit, "I Came Back to Say Good-bye," and next he sang "Heartless Woman."

Jenifer and I were at Dad's table, and I was trying to get Dad's eye, trying to tell him some way, *Hey, Pop, you pulled it off! You did it!* But Dad was watching him, nodding a little to the music, a smile at the corners of his lips.

When Chooch was through with the two songs, he said over the applause, "Let me eat in peace now, or no more music!"

The church ladies came hurrying out of the kitchen with hot chicken and mashed for him, and biscuits and gravy, and most of us helped ourselves to seconds to keep Chooch company.

"This is my son, Ted," my father said.

Chooch said, "Chip off the old block?"

My father nodded.

Then Chooch said to me, "Lord, I hope not! I hope you're not the stuffed shirt your old man was in high school."

I saw Dad's eyes blink while I tried to think of an answer to that.

Under her breath, Jenifer said, "That's not nice."

Chooch wolfed down the chicken, mouth open while he chewed, and told everybody, "I couldn't believe Pastor Snore was on the horn to me. I told my manager: This I gotta see! This guy was a dead head in school, and I don't mean he followed around after the Grateful Dead. He was a dead head." Chooch let his head drop on his shoulder, acting out what he was saying.

The kids were laughing.

"Of course, Edward, here—we always called him Edward. He was no Eddie, were you, Edward? Edward here probably never expected I'd turn up at his place for any reason other than to ask for a loan, or ask him to hide me from the law or something nefarious. How do you like that word—*nefarious*? You like it, Edward?"

"It's a good word," my father said quietly.

"It's the way you think of me, probably. I haven't changed, either, if that's what you thought. There's no God in my blanking life, and thank you, Taylor Train, for saying 'blanking.' When we all know what I *really* mean."

The kids at our table were exchanging puzzled looks.

My mother said, "We really appreciate your coming out of your way to do this for us."

"So you're the gal who married Snore?" Chooch said.

"I'm happy to say I am," said my mother.

"Happy to say she is," said Chooch, and then he dropped his head to his shoulder and made a snoring sound.

By the time he got up to do two more songs, Jenifer was whispering that he was a pig, not worthy of sitting at my father's feet, much less at his table.

There were four kids sitting there who'd heard Chooch. He'd barely taken a breath between insults aimed at Dad. The kids had grown quiet, and their smiles had faded as they began to realize that for some reason Chooch was bent on humiliating

Dad. Mom was looking down at her lap, mostly, and Dad was looking straight ahead.

Everybody else in the place was up on their feet, arms in the air, hands fisted, crying out happily, "Whoa! Whoa!" at the end of each number, whistling, squealing. They had gotten what they'd come for.

I'll never know what made Chooch do four more numbers than he'd announced, or what made him take questions and sign autographs. I'll never know why he agreed to come at all.

Mom thought perhaps it was an attempt to soften his image, since he had seen to it that the next day newspapers would report his good deed.

Dad said that maybe he identified with the kids: the ones who couldn't afford the big dinner dance, the ones who weren't coupled, the loners, the cynics, the outsiders. You should have seen their faces that night. You should have seen Cal, Peter, Leary, and Judge!

Chooch even tossed Ellie Tutton his cap . . . which took guts because his hair was thinning.

All the kids were following him out the door except the ones at our table.

"He was mean to you, Reverend," Billy Tonsetter said.

"He makes jokes, Billy."

"He's not *all* bad," Mom said.

"I don't like him anymore, though," said Jenifer. "He's not respectful."

"No, he's not," Dad said. "But he kept his word."

I thought about that evening forever.

I'll think forever about that evening.

My father must have known that anyone who wrote that in his yearbook, who had become a nefarious (thanks, Chooch) rock singer not known for his gentle demeanor, could probably not be counted on to behave politely toward a man of the cloth he'd never taken to when he was a boy.

My father must have known what he'd be up against with Chooch, as surely as he'd known the only way to rescue the outsiders after the graduation ceremony was to get Chooch there . . . somehow.

And Dad did.

Choo Choo Train kept his word . . . and then more.

And my father, in my eyes that evening, became my hero again . . . and then more.

I'm the same unbeliever that I was before I went off to New York, but I know what grace is now . . . and I try for that.

I try to be like Dad.

Jess Mowry

Pogo trudged wearily to the truck and hoisted the big burlap sack off his shoulders. It thudded against the others he'd loaded and puffed out a cloud of white dust. At forty-five kilos, or one hundred pounds, each sack weighed nearly as much as he did; and he paused to lean, panting, against the tailgate and wipe the gray sweat from his ebony face. He was almost thirteen, solid but slender, with every small muscle tightly defined under skin the shade of a panther at midnight, but striped like a zebra with sweat streaks and dust. He wore only cutoffs, so ragged and low that they bared his lean hips like a loincloth with pockets and seemed to be more decoration than clothes. A slim strip of leather encircled his neck, and a silver charm glittered against his chest as he ruffled the dust from his hair.

The hot Haitian sun was a blazing brass ball as it sank

toward the shimmering sea in the west; and Pogo turned toward it, spreading his arms to welcome the cool evening breeze. The truck was parked on a small flat space at the rim of an ancient volcano. Seabirds circled and soared overhead, snowy white in brilliant blue, calling and probably cursing at Pogo for still being there when they wanted to land. Deep inside the volcano's cone was a miniature lake that mirrored the sky, surrounded by vine-tangled trees. Eastward lay most of the tiny island, only a few square miles in size; and much of that was used to grow crops—beans, plantains, and sugarcane.

Despite his fatigue from working since dawn, digging, sacking, and loading guano, Pogo wiped the dust from his eyes and took a long moment to look around. He'd read many books about other lands, and seen lots of pictures in old magazines, but nowhere on earth seemed as pretty a place as his own little island of Cayes Squellette. Far away on the distant horizon was the pale silhouette of a passenger ship, probably bound for Kingston, Jamaica, with a cargo of people in deck chairs aboard. Closer to shore was a big motor yacht; but few foreign tourists visited Haiti, and no one came to Skeleton Cay.

Below the cliffs, a small open boat with a tattered brown sail was tacking carefully through the reefs on a southeastern course for the island's cove. Iris Millay was at the tiller, while André DeFoe kept a lookout ahead. Pogo shaded his eyes from the fiery sun and watched as Iris guided the boat through a foaming gap in the black lava teeth. To sail inshore was the fastest way home but a foolish and dangerous thing to do; and André, at least, was supposed to know better. Pogo hoped that Esu was with them, watching until the boat cleared the rocks and reached deeper water in safety. He whispered a prayer and shook his head, then walked to a shack made of plywood and tin.

Inside were stacks of burlap bags and a battered old scale to weigh them on. There was also a wooden table and chair, and another boy of about Pogo's age sat asleep in the chair with his feet on the table and his fingers laced over his stomach. He was very round and rolly fat, with a cheerfully chubby-cheeked, button-nosed face and a mane of hair as wild as Pogo's but only lightly dusted with white. He covered more of his cutoff jeans than the cutoffs covered him, and he wore the same little silver medallion between the jiggly shapes of his chest.

Pogo smiled, recalling pictures he'd seen in books of fat little children with angel wings who were painted on ceilings in Catholic churches. "Laurent!" he called. "How many is that?"

"Huh? . . . Oh." The other boy opened his eyes and yawned, then reached for a shabby old notebook. "How many did you load after lunch?"

"*Ven,*" said Pogo, Kreyol for twenty.

Laurent got a pencil and added up numbers. "*Senkant,*" he said with satisfaction. "Fifty sacks we have loaded today while the men are at work on the schooner. She will have a full cargo after all, and my father will be pleased." He flipped through the pages. "And I have written a poem. About you, *mwen frè.* Listen."

Pogo came into the shade, his bare feet raising puffs of dust that haunted his ankles like baby ghosts. A half-empty water jug stood on the table, along with the palm leaf wrappers of lunch—curried goat, plantains, and rice. Laurent offered Pogo a drink from the jug, then took one himself and cleared his throat:

> "Shape of a cheetah, heart of a lion,
>> black as a panther under the sun.
> Brave as a leopard, strong as a tiger,
>> fleet as a jaguar on the run."

He paused expectantly. "What do you think?"

"It's very . . . um . . . catty," said Pogo, then asked, "Is that all?"

"It's not finished yet," said Laurent. "Poetry is difficult work. But do you like it so far?"

"Well, I'm not sure about 'leopard brave' and 'lion heart.'"

Pogo looked down at himself. "But you have made me very handsome."

Laurent smiled slyly. "Iris Millay thinks this about you."

Pogo frowned. "Where did you hear that?"

Laurent only grinned. "Privileged information, Lieutenant."

"She has a strange way of showing it," Pogo muttered. "She called me Flying Fox Face yesterday."

"Girls are like that, my brother. It is not what they say, but that they say something." Laurent tossed the notebook back on the table.

"Don't leave it there please," said Pogo. "Someone might read it."

"Maybe Iris Millay?" Laurent chuckled. "But I have not used your name."

"Only you write poetry, Laurent. And Iris Millay is no fool." Then Pogo added, "Even if she dares the reef to save a few foolish minutes."

"She did?" asked Laurent. "And when?"

"Just now."

"I will speak to her about that. I will not have our fishing boat risked."

"Um," asked Pogo, "will you tell your father?"

"That won't be necessary. But wasn't André in command?"

"It is hard to command Iris Millay."

"Watch me, Lieutenant. But maybe you're right about the poem." Laurent recovered the notebook, tore out a page and folded it carefully into his pocket, then glanced toward the sea at the lowering sun. "We have time for a swim before supper." He studied Pogo and chuckled again. "You look like a *zonbi* who was buried in guano instead of a proper grave."

Pogo sighed and stretched his muscles. "I feel like a *zonbi*. Fifty sacks has been no fun, even with you to help."

"I think you have broken André's record."

"I think I do not really care." Pogo went back to the truck and closed the wooden tailgate. The vehicle was the color of rust, a 1923 Linn, with big iron tracks like a bulldozer instead of a set of rear wheels. Its cab was open like a jeep's, there wasn't any windshield, and its front tires were worn completely smooth, displaying fabric all around. RHINOCEROS was painted in yellow on either side of the hood.

Laurent slid from the chair and followed Pogo. "I'll help you start it."

"Thanks," said Pogo. "The magneto contacts are burned. Maybe my father can find a new set when he sails to Port-au-Prince. Advance the spark and give it half throttle."

"Be careful, Lieutenant. Rhino could break your arm again."

Pogo laughed and flexed a bicep as big and round as a

baseball. "My arm is stronger now." He patted the rusty fender. "Hear that, you *bastaèd*? Do not give me grief." He helped Laurent climb into the cab by putting a shoulder beneath his bottom and hoisting him like a guano sack. Laurent squeezed behind the big steering wheel with his chest overlapping the rim, flipped a switch, adjusted two levers, then stepped on the clutch and shifted to neutral. "Ready for takeoff, Lieutenant."

Pogo went to the front of the truck, where a heavy crank handle stuck out from under the radiator. "Wake up, beast!" He grabbed the handle and twisted it over. The engine caught with a sudden roar, but Laurent immediately cut the throttle and retarded the spark before it could backfire. It settled into a slow-thumping idle while puffing out clouds of blue-tinted smoke. Pogo came to the driver's side and saluted Laurent. "We make a good team, *mwen Chéf*."

"I'm not your chief yet," corrected Laurent. "The people will make that choice for themselves when my father decides to retire."

"But for three hundred years it has been the same choice, and Cayes Squellette has always prospered."

"Thank you, loyal subject. But I have not even come of age yet, so nothing is certain, and eggs are not chickens."

Pogo climbed onto the running board. "Your ceremony is four days away, and you will make everyone proud." He scanned Laurent's face, then asked, "Have I said something wrong?"

"*Non.* I just think about it a lot. And more as my birthday approaches."

"We all do that," said Pogo. "A lot before, and . . . according to my father . . . a lifetime after. Would you like to drive?"

"You may." Laurent squirmed out from behind the wheel and scooted across the dusty seat, which was only a board covered with canvas and thinly padded with straw.

Pogo slid into the driver's position, adjusted the spark, and lowered the throttle. He trod the clutch and shifted to first while giving the engine more gas. The truck billowed smoke and clattered away. Its iron tracks squealed and clanked on the rock as it reached the rim and began the descent. The grade was steep as the trail curved down toward the little blue lake with its circle of forest; and Pogo kept the truck in low gear because the brakes were badly worn. The air grew cooler as they reached the trees, but Pogo was shiny and dripping with sweat from fighting the massive steering wheel, which jerked and twisted to and fro as the truck lumbered over the rocky terrain. The trail leveled off to round the lake, and Pogo shifted to second. The truck now followed the ruts it had made; and Pogo took his hands off the wheel to wipe the guano mud out of his eyes. "Would you like to stop here and swim?"

Laurent lounged back with his feet on the dash and his arms behind his head. "Esu's pool is better. The water is always fresh from falling, as if it gathers life from the air. And I want to talk with Him."

"About your ceremony?" asked Pogo. "Why do you worry? No boy or girl has ever failed."

"I do not worry, I just think a lot. . . . My rowing is not as good as yours."

"You row as well as anyone. But we could practice if you want."

"That's a good idea."

The truck clattered on beneath towering trees, leaving a trail of smoke in its wake. Sunlight shafted through the leaves, golden now at late afternoon. Bright-colored birds flew squawking and screaming, disturbed by the rumble and clanking below. Pogo downshifted to first gear again, and the truck clawed its way to the top of the rim, balanced there for a breathless moment, then dropped its nose with a bone-shaking crash and descended toward the fringe of forest that still surrounded the mountain. Pogo used both feet on the brake, producing a teeth-gritting screech from the tracks but barely slowing them down.

"I hate this part," muttered Laurent as he clung to the top of the dashboard. "If people were meant to go this fast, then Esu would have given us wings!"

They bucked and jolted down the slope at twenty miles an hour. The trail veered south at the foot of the mountain, muddy and soft under silkcotton trees that had never been cut in three hundred years. The tires sank down to their rusty rims, and the rattling tracks threw mud everywhere, including on both of the boys. They passed the little village graveyard, with timber crosses and lava headstones painted in colors of every hue that rivaled the flowers growing there and the butterflies dancing above. Candles flickered in mason jars and in various bottles and vases. Over the rattle and clatter of iron came the low rushing roar of a small waterfall. Laurent appeared to be napping again, but asked without opening his eyes, "You are thinking about your mother?"

"*Wi*," said Pogo, glancing back at the peaceful graveyard. "It has been two years since the hurricane, but I still miss her very much." He turned to Laurent. "Do you think she will see my ceremony? And the part I will play in yours?"

"I think she will. But ask Jeanette Millay." Then Laurent smiled. "Or Iris. She too will be a *mambo* someday."

Pogo shrugged. "We used to talk of many things, Iris and I. But, now she seems preoccupied, and silly at other times. . . . I don't think she likes me anymore."

"Her ceremony is soon after yours. Perhaps that occupies her mind."

Pogo nodded. "Maybe." Then he added, "I catch more fish than André."

"I am aware of that. But I needed your strength to load the guano."

"André is stronger than me."

"You already know how to fish."

The truck lumbered on through deepening shadows. Its lights had burned out before Pogo was born, but Pogo knew the way by heart and ducked the occasional low-hanging vines that dangled like sinuous snakes from the trees. The soothing rush of falling water now became the only sound as they rounded the southeastern foot of the mountain and stopped near a rippling pool, which was thickly encircled by broad-leaf ferns and shadowed by coconut palms. The fall tumbled over a black lava cliff to fling up streamers of swirling spray and shroud the pool in drifting mist. Pogo switched off the engine. "We need an offering."

Laurent pulled the poem from his pocket. "I have this."

"But it's about me."

"Are you not one of His creations?"

The boys got down and slipped out of their cutoffs. Laurent plucked a leaf, rolled the paper up in it, and tucked it tightly into his hair. Then he and Pogo pushed through the ferns and waded out into the water. Pogo swam, silent and slenderly graceful, while Laurent came paddling noisily after. Pogo submerged to wash off the dust, scaring small fish as he glided along, then surfaced and waited for Laurent to catch up. Reaching the fall, the boys took deep breaths and plunged underneath. It was like passing from one world into another— a moment's journey of swirling confusion, and then they emerged in a green-lit grotto, lushly lined with velvety moss like the emerald womb of a forest. The fading rays of the setting sun filtered through the falling water to play about in shimmers and sparkles and shifting ribbons of rainbow. Mist filled the cave like the haze of a dream. A candle burned in an ancient lantern; and here and there around the walls were shadowed hollows deep in the rock where skulls looked out and smiled.

The naked form of a jet-black boy sat upon a carpet of moss, lounging back against the wall and surrounded by glistening ferns. His knees were up and widely spread, and He rested a hand on top of a tummy so huge and round that it looked like a planet. He seemed to be about eight years old, an ordinary Haitian boy with the chubby face of a mischievous imp who'd gotten remarkably fat—if you didn't consider the prominent pair of baby goat horns on His woolly-maned head. His other hand held a bottle of rum; and piled around His tremendous tummy were offerings of every kind—seashells, marbles, pretty pebbles, a plastic party-favor trumpet, a pocket-knife, a model boat, various coins, and other things a boy His age would probably like. There were also bottles of island-brewed beer; and at His side within easy reach was a bowl of rice and pork. A cigar was clamped in His grinning teeth, and others lay in a box nearby. Esu was carved from ebony wood, but He seemed to cheerfully wink at His guests as if He knew why they had come. Pogo's mouth watered as he scented the food; and Esu seemed to grin even wider, as if He remembered when eight-year-old Pogo had shared His meals and sipped His beer. Laurent and Pogo climbed out of the water to greet the boy-god with reverent *bon soir*s and kneel at His feet in the moss.

"Do you think I should read it to Him?" Laurent whispered.

"A poem *is* meant to be read, you know." Then Pogo giggled. "And why do you whisper, *enbesil*? Do you think He can't hear your thoughts?"

Laurent read his poem, and Esu's black eyes seemed to sparkle. Laurent rolled the paper back up in the leaf and laid it near Esu's toes. Pogo waited with lowered head while Laurent prepared to make his request. He was almost shocked to hear Laurent ask, "Please, Esu, make me strong and brave like Pogo."

Pogo opened one eye to see if Laurent was joking—Esu loved jokes and often played them—but Laurent's chubby face was serious. Praying to Esu and giving Him gifts was no guarantee He would actually help you—He *was* only eight and might just forget. Laurent reached out to rub Esu's tummy, which was polished as smooth as an onyx mirror by generations of children's hands. Pogo rose to his feet with Laurent, then took Laurent's shoulders and studied his face. Out on earth it was nearly dark; and only the candle lit the grotto, striking gold sparks in Laurent's dripping hair and reflecting from his silver medallion.

"I don't understand," said Pogo. "You're already strong and brave."

Laurent shook his head. "I have never been hurt. Your arm was broken, and . . ." He touched a small scar on Pogo's side. "That street boy stabbed you in Port-au-Prince."

Pogo shrugged. "Hunger makes people do desperate things."

"But it must have hurt a lot."

"As my father said then, you do not collect pain like souvenirs. Nor do you hoard it away like money, because it can buy you nothing. You hurt for a while and then it is gone. You can't remember pain, except that it hurt, and maybe a lot, and you pray it will never hurt again." Pogo paused to think. "And if your heart has learned from its pain, you also pray it will never hurt for anyone else as much it it hurt for you."

Laurent gripped Pogo's hard-muscled arms. "I'm glad you're strong, *mwen frè*."

Pogo searched Laurent's eyes in the candle glow. "Why should that matter?"

"Don't you know?"

Pogo thought for another moment. "*Wi*. I guess I do." He flexed a bicep and smiled. "Is this why I have been digging guano?"

"Are you angry with me?"

Pogo laughed and hugged Laurent. "How could I be? You have made me into a handsome poem and then offered me to Esu."

Laurent returned the hug. "Come then, Lieutenant. Supper is waiting."

They said *bon soir* to Esu, then slipped back into the roiling water, dove beneath the roaring fall, and surfaced beyond in the pool. A slim silver crescent of newly born moon hung in the sky like a smile overhead. Night birds called from deep in the forest, and bats flitted silently through the trees. The boys returned to the truck and dressed; then Pogo boosted Laurent aboard. This time it didn't start easily, and Pogo cranked for several minutes while cursing many things to hell. At last the engine sputtered to life.

"I will drive now," said Laurent. "You rest, *mwen frè*."

"As you wish, *mwen Chéf*," panted Pogo, crawling up onto the seat.

Laurent let out the clutch, and the truck clattered on. He quickly upshifted to second, then third. A brook meandered from Esu's pool, down to the cove where the village lay. The trail crossed the water several times, the truck splashing through and flinging up spray that hissed and steamed on the hot radiator. Pogo opened an eye and laughed. "If people were meant to go this fast, then Esu would have given us wings."

Laurent ducked a bat as big as a fox. "If people were meant to miss their suppers, then no one would cook them, *enbesil!*"

The village was only a dozen houses scattered about under trees. They were various sizes and ages, the oldest of logs and heavy timber, the newer of plywood and packing-crate planks. All were raised on stones or blocks, roofed with rusty sheets of tin; and their porches were wide and meant to be used for sitting and playing and long conversations. Their windows had screens instead of glass, with shutters to close against storms.

The scents of cooking filled the air—rice and beans, fried plantains, and the rich aromas of goat and pork. The soft glow of candles and kerosene lamps shone out from windows and doorways. Barefoot women in colorful dresses were visiting neighbors to borrow or trade this or that for a meal—a pinch of spice, a handful of peppers. Children played hide-and-seek in the shadows, chickens were flapping to roost in the trees, and model boats raced in the rippling brook. The younger kids wore only their charms, the older boys were in cutoffs or shorts, and the older girls were dressed the same except for tank tops or tees. Pogo waved to André DeFoe, who puffed a cigar on the steps of his porch. He was newly fourteen and solidly muscled, and was reading a book by lantern light. Laurent stopped the truck and asked, "How many fish today, *mwen frè*?"

"Two baskets," said André.

"*Bon.* But try for three tomorrow. . . . And if you set out a little earlier, you won't have to cross the western reef to make it home before dark."

"That was not my idea," André protested.

"A captain is responsible for the safety of those aboard his ship."

André considered, then nodded. "I had not thought of that."

Laurent drove on through the village, and the younger kids ran to climb aboard for a short ride down to the cove. Laurent's little brother, Tomas, was with them, and the silver charm was all he wore. He was eight like Esu, with an impish grin, a jungle of hair, and a tummy almost as round and huge. Laurent stopped again, and Pogo got down to boost him into the passenger seat. "The schooner is ready," puffed Tomas. "They are pushing her into the water now."

"*Bon,*" said Laurent. "She can sail as soon as the guano is loaded."

The largest house in the tiny village wasn't the chief's but belonged to the *mambo*, and was also the island's schoolroom. Iris Millay and Simone Devereaux were doing their homework out on the steps, where a candle burned in a little shrine. Iris wore shorts and a faded blue tank top, clinging tightly to her dusky young body. Her hair was an ebony halo of curls above eyes with a hint of gold in their depths. She seemed to be watching as Pogo rode past—on the running board because of Tomas—although she pretended not to.

"See what I mean?" said Pogo. "She will not even look at me, dammit."

Laurent only smiled. "Staring is rude. It is something you do to people you *don't* like."

"I had not thought of that. . . . Um, are you going to speak to her?"

"I already have. Through André."

"Oh. I see." Pogo nodded. "It is truly in your blood to be chief."

"*Non,* Lieutenant. Those are only skills to be learned, like fishing or sailing or driving this truck." Laurent waved to Simone. She was cocoa brown and a little bit chubby, in red cotton shorts and a yellow T-shirt, with a schoolbook balanced on her knee.

"Simone looked at you," said Pogo.

"*Wi.* But she did not stare."

"Oh."

They rattled through a grove of palms and emerged on a white-sanded beach. The forty-foot schooner was almost afloat, rolling on logs with a dozen men pushing. "Everyone help!" ordered Laurent, and the children ran to add their shoulders. The new copper sheets on the schooner's bottom gleamed in the glow of gasoline lanterns set here and there in the sand; and in minutes the vessel was floating free.

Pogo could never quite decide if Joseph Latortue, Laurent's father, reminded him more of a sumo wrestler or a mighty statue of Buddha. He wore only tan shorts, the small silver charm, and steel-rimmed spectacles low on his nose. He stood knee-deep in the moonlit water, talking with Pogo's father, Paul, a muscular man with the cheetah-like build of his son.

". . . Gasoline, and another barrel of oil for the truck," Joseph was saying.

"*Wi, mwen Chéf,*" said Paul. He studied the schooner to

see how she floated. "I will check for leaks while the crew goes to supper. Then we'll load her, sail by midnight, and should be back on Tuesday morning. Wind and Esu willing."

Pogo waded out to his father and got a sweaty hug. "Don't forget the magneto parts. Rhino is getting very moody."

"Pogo and I loaded fifty more sacks," announced Laurent.

Joseph smiled and embraced his son, enveloping him in hugeness. "A good day's work." He gave Pogo a wink. "Both of you must be tired."

"Hungry mostly," said Laurent. "I invited Pogo to eat with us. Then we're going to—"

The beach was suddenly lit bright as day, as the blue-white beam of a powerful seachlight stabbed across the water. Joseph shaded his eyes with a hand and looked to the rocky jaws of the cove. "Now, what is that? Not a government gunboat, I hope. I thought those days were past."

Pogo's father faced the glare as the searchlight probed for a way through the rocks. "A gunboat would probably wait until morning. The last one to try got stuck on the reef and had to be rescued by a tug." He laughed. "A Dominican tug . . . They were not pleased."

"I saw a motor yacht," said Pogo. "From up on the mountain an hour ago. It seemed to be heading this way, but I didn't think it was coming here."

"Well, it seems to be trying. Take the longboat and guide it in. Hurry before there's a wreck."

"Come on, Laurent," said Pogo, grabbing a lantern to signal with. "Now is a good time to practice your rowing."

"I'm coming too!" said Tomas.

"Run get the rifle," ordered Laurent. "In case they are smugglers or pirates."

A short time later the gleaming white yacht, twice the size of the Cayes Squellette schooner, let go its anchor within the small cove like an iron fist through liquid crystal. Its port-holes and windows blazed with light that lit up the water all around and brought curious fish to the surface. Laurent pulled the oars of the twenty-foot longboat and squinted up at the varnished decks. "Electric lights are too damn bright."

"I guess people get used to them," said Pogo. He held the rifle, a massive old thing as long as he was tall, with a wooden stock that covered the barrel all the way to the tip.

"Then they must forget what night is like. As if it was something to scare away."

"Blanc," said Tomas, as two white men in cotton trousers and polo shirts came out on deck to check the anchor. Pogo studied them with interest: He hadn't seen many *blanc* in his life, and only in Port-au-Prince. "They do not look like smugglers to me."

"These days it is hard to tell," said Laurent. "Ready your rifle and see what they do."

"Shall I aim it at them?"

"No need to be rude."

Pogo cocked the heavy bolt, and its omnious clack echoed over the water. The men exchanged uncertain glances and moved away from the rail.

Laurent smiled. "Well done, Lieutenant. I assume they speak French."

"I doubt they speak Kreyol," said Pogo.

"Bonsoir," called Laurent, using the French pronunciation. "Welcome to Cayes Squellette."

"Bonsoir," answered one of the men. He seemed surprised to hear Laurent's French, and his own was far from perfect. The rifle obviously made him nervous, although it was aimed at the stars. "Thank you for guiding us in." He looked to be in his early forties, with sandy-blond hair and a neatly trimmed beard. He glanced at the rifle again. "May I speak with your elder or chief? Or is this not a proper time?"

"I'm the chief's son," said Laurent. "We were just about to have supper. I am sure that my father would enjoy your company. I can take you ashore if you wish."

"Thank you." The blond man conferred with the other, older, whose brown hair and beard were sprinkled with gray.

They spoke in English, Pogo noted, debating whether to come with the boys or to use their own launch. Pogo heard the word *etiquette*—it *was* the chief's son who had offered to row them. The blond man leaned over the rail. "We will follow you in our own boat, so you won't have to row us back."

Laurent grinned at Pogo and said in Kreyol, "How tactful."

The men went aft to lower their skiff, but Pogo noticed a door swing open under the pilot house. A sleepy-looking boy appeared. He was close to being Pogo's age, with a shaggy mop of silver-blond hair that almost completely covered his eyes. His chubby tummy lapped over his jeans, which seemed rather shabby and tightly outgrown for a boy so apparently rich. They barely managed to cling to his hips as he yawned and stretched in the doorway.

"I've never seen a young *blanc* before," said Tomas. "Except in magazine pictures."

"Nor have I," said Pogo. He compared the clothes of the men and the boy, and added, "Perhaps he is a crewman."

"Perhaps," agreed Laurent. "But do not stare. It's rude." He glanced to the shore. "The entire village has come out to see, so everyone's supper is waiting now."

Joseph Latortue, in fresh khaki shorts and matching shirt, stood on his porch to greet the guests as Laurent escorted them up from the beach. Pogo and Tomas followed behind, the rifle slung over Pogo's shoulder. The blond boy seemed to be more than a crewman, because he had come along. He had put on a T-shirt and Nikes, but the shoes were battered and the shirt too small.

The house's front room was partly an office, with an antique desk and a file cabinet where various papers and records were kept. On the wall were a picture of Haiti's new president and a government paper that gave Laurent's father the power to excecute people—though in three hundred years this had never happened. Joseph briefly described his duties as he ushered the visitors into the kitchen. Pogo unslung the heavy rifle, ejected the bullet, put it back in the clip, then stood the weapon by the door.

". . . Settle disputes," Joseph was saying as Pogo came into the kitchen. "Preside at weddings performed by our *mambo,* fill out birth and death certificates, send copies to Port-au-Prince once a year. And keep records of our enterprise, which is exporting guano aboard the schooner." He took his place at the head of the table, which had been reset with a red linen cloth and the ancient formal dishes. Candles burned in pewter stands, and a gasoline lantern hung overhead. Laurent's mother had changed to her best gingham dress and had put fresh flowers in mason jars. Joseph waved everyone into chairs. "This is my wife, Angélique. You have met my sons,

Laurent and Tomas. And this is Pogo Malroux."

"My name is David Benson," said the blond man. "This is my associate, Robert MacRae." He glanced at the blond boy, who still looked sleepy. "And my son, Randy. We're from America."

"North, South, or Central?" asked Laurent.

"Er . . ." said David, "the United States."

Pogo had been studying Randy while trying to be polite about it. Like the men he was tanned to a coppery tone—at least the visible parts of him—showing he'd spent lots of time at sea. His eyes were bright blue beneath his pale hair; and his face looked potentially cheerful, though maybe he wasn't in the mood right now. He appeared to be waking up a bit; and if he thought his surroundings were strange, he was good at not letting on. He seemed accustomed to candles, and looked as if he trusted his nose that the food would be worth waking up for. Joseph had also been scanning the boy, as if more could be learned from him than from the men.

"You are, perhaps, missionaries?" asked Joseph.

The blond man smiled as if at a joke. "No. I'm a writer. And Robert is a photographer. We've done a series of books on religions, and we're working on one about voodoo now . . . real voodoo. Not the Hollywood movie stuff."

Joseph seemed relieved: missionaries, as he'd often said,

were usually a pain in the butt, always overstaying their welcome and never shutting up, as if Jesus Christ preferred pushy people to annoy the world in His name. "Ah. No sticking of pins into dolls, or calling up *zonbis* from graves."

"Yes," said David, seeming also relieved that Joseph had a sense of humor. "And we heard about a coming-of-age ceremony unique to your island."

"As a matter of fact, my son will be having his next week. You are welcome to stay and observe. Or to even take part if you wish. I will introduce you to our *mambo,* Jeanette Millay."

"Er," said David, "you have no . . . *oungan*, no priest?"

Joseph laughed. "*Voodu* is an equal-opportunity religion. But you must be hungry after your voyage. Laurent, will you pass the plantains? Tomas, pour the wine, please."

Laurent nudged Pogo and whispered, *"Finally!"*

Pogo watched Randy. He seemed to be fully awake now; and if a naked Haitian eight-year-old pouring French wine was any surprise, he was too polite to show it. What was the English word . . . *cool*?

Tomas's charm lay atop his huge tummy instead of dangling down, and David seemed to be studying it as the boy came over and filled his glass. "May I?"

Tomas smiled and spread his arms. "Of course."

David took the charm in his hand and examined the design.

It depicted a boy who looked like Tomas sitting atop a pile of skulls—except of course that the boy had horns. "Interesting," said David. "I've seen this theme in other religions."

"It is the circle," said Joseph. "Of life and death, and then life anew."

"In *heaven*?" asked David, smiling slightly. "Or beginning again as a child?"

"Does it not say in the Christian Bible, Unless you become as a little child, you shall not enter into the kingdom of heaven?"

"Interesting. I noticed when we came ashore that everyone seems to wear these. Are they of African origin?"

"Esu is of African origin," said Joseph, drawing Tomas to his side. "The charms are manufactured in China." He chuckled. "The same company also makes Catholic crucifixes, Egyptian ankhs, and statues of Buddha and Krishna." He ruffled Tomas's hair. "But after all, it is God whom we worship, and not His image on chrome-plated brass. Those are only reminders." He glanced at Randy. "Like carrying a picture of those you love."

After supper Laurent and Pogo excused themselves and went out on the porch with bottles of beer. Tomas had tried to escape with them when Jeanette Millay had come over, but had been recaptured to do the dishes. Laurent lay back against the rail, unbuttoned his cutoffs and patted his stomach. "It was worth the wait." He happily sighed. "My mother must have borrowed something from everyone in the village."

"*Wi,*" agreed Pogo, his own tummy round and tight as a drum as he settled comfortably on the steps. "I thought I tasted Jeanette's curry sauce and Madame Devereaux's chicken in wine." He took a sip of beer and burped. "*Pardon-moi.* Do you want to practice rowing?"

"Maybe later. I'm too full now. We should have guests more often."

"I will drink to that." Pogo gazed toward the cove. The schooner was being loaded with the last of the sacks from the truck. It seemed strange to see the lights of the yacht, painfully and unnaturally bright. The screen door squeaked, and Randy came out. He hadn't said much during supper, though his appetite had spoken volumes. Pogo smiled and scooted over to offer a place on the steps. "Hi," he said.

"Hi," said Randy. "I didn't know you guys could speak English."

"Is *duh* an English word?" said Laurent.

"Only a little," Pogo answered. "Jeanette Millay teaches English at school, and we have a community radio."

"You surprised my dad," said Randy. "I guess he thought you were savage or something."

"We will eat you tomorrow." Laurent giggled. "We are just too full right now."

"I can relate," said Randy, lifting his wobbly roll of stomach to show his unzipped jeans. "My dad ain't much of a cook. An' Robert could burn a potful of water. I mostly microwave stuff on the boat, an' this's been the best dinner in months."

"Would you like a beer?" asked Pogo.

"Thought you'd never ask."

"In the chest over there. Please help yourself."

"Is this a pirate's chest?" asked Randy, opening the massive lid. "It looks like one I saw in a movie."

"It is in a way," said Laurent.

Randy took out a bottle and tried to twist off the cap. Pogo laughed. "It is not that kind. We cap them ourselves with a hand machine. Use the lock on the chest to open it."

Randy sat down and took a sip, and then a great big gulp. "Whoa! This's way better than Heineken!"

"It is our island recipe," said Laurent. "The secret is sugarcane."

Randy pushed the hair out of his eyes. "I thought beer had to be cold to taste good."

"I had a cold Budweiser in Port-au-Prince," said Pogo. "I did not think it tasted good."

"Yeah," said Randy, drinking deeply. "When we were in

England, my dad asked a waitress for an American beer, an' she called it 'fairy piss'!"

"Have you been all over the world?" asked Laurent.

"A few places . . . Africa, India, Tibet, Burma, Iran. Central an' South America. Like you heard, my dad writes books about religions. It was Druids in England. They worship trees." He paused to wipe the sweat from his face. "Funny, but most of the coolest religions seem to be in the hottest places."

"You can take off your shirt if you want," said Pogo. "We are not very formal on Cayes Squellette." He prodded Laurent, who might as well have been naked. "As you may have already noticed."

"Thanks," said Randy, peeling out of his tee. His body was tan all over, but soft as coconut pudding. "We got air-conditioning on the boat. Spoils you, I guess. I read a lot in a deck chair outside. An' drink a lot of beer." He patted his stomach. "But you probably figured that already."

"Beware of our beer," said Laurent. "Or you will soon look like Tomas."

Pogo smiled. "I was looking at you because I have never seen a young *blanc* before."

Randy spread his arms. "Ta-da! I'm not shy. Been too many places where people don't even wear clothes." He kicked off his shoes to show his tan feet as if to confirm that fact.

"How old are you?" asked Laurent.

"Be thirteen in August. The seventh."

"Cool!" said Pogo. "That is my birthday, too."

"Whoa! That is kinda cool. Are you gonna have a voodoo thing?"

"*Voodu. Wi* . . . yes. Though it is Laurent who is being honored now."

"Are you gonna stick pins in him?"

"Of course not."

Randy took another drink and glanced over his shoulder. "Well, my dad's probably gonna be in there all night, askin' a million questions. You'll probably *want* to put him in a pot if he stays for a week. He almost got our heads cut off in Brazil by insulting a shaman."

"Well," said Pogo, "we can sit out here until dawn if we like. But what is your own religion, Randy?"

"I don't got one."

"You do not believe in God?" asked Laurent, sitting up.

Randy drank what was left in his bottle. "Maybe I've seen too many, an' none of 'em seem to do nothin' for nobody."

"That is terrible English," said Pogo.

"Would you like to meet God?" asked Laurent.

"Huh? You're kiddin', right?"

"Of course not."

"Oh. You mean like see your church or your shrine or something? No offense, bro, but I seen tons of those already."

"Well," said Laurent. "Esu does have an *ounphor* . . . a shrine . . . but He is real."

"Aw, everybody's god is *real* to them."

"There is only one God," said Pogo. "But He has many forms and faces, just like the people He created."

Randy shrugged. "Okay. So let's see yours."

Laurent pointed to the cove. "The truck is unloaded. Bring it up here, Lieutenant." He got to his feet and buttoned his cutoffs, then went to the chest. "I'll get some offerings."

"Come and meet Rhino," said Pogo.

"Is he a god, too?" asked Randy.

"He thinks he is."

Randy started to get up but plopped down again. "Whoa!" he giggled. "You were right about your beer! It's somethin' to beware of!"

Pogo took him under the arms and helped him to his feet. "That is okay, *mwen frè* . . . my bro," he said with a glance at Laurent. "Like Rhino, I am a beast of burden."

Laurent went into the house and returned with a shiny new charm. Pogo held Randy around the waist, steadying him, as Laurent tied the leather strip.

"Do I need this to meet God?" asked Randy, admiring the medallion.

"*Non,*" said Pogo. "It is only a gift from us."

"Thanks. It's cool. I got painted blue somewhere up the Amazon. It was a ritual sacrifice."

"How strange," said Laurent. "Who would sacrifice children?"

In the kitchen Jeanette Millay, a powerful woman in a calico dress, with beaded bracelets and seashell necklaces, was patiently puffing her wooden pipe and answering David's questions. Angélique was pouring coffee, while Tomas stood on a box at the sink and dutifully washed the dishes. Joseph smoked a Cuban cigar, as did the older man, Robert. David was taking notes on a laptop. "But isn't Esu a minor god?" He tapped keys to call up an image, then glanced at Tomas as if to compare them. "An eight-year-old boy with horns? Like on your medallions?"

"To some he is minor," said Jeanette. "Merely an imp, or perhaps the equivalent of a Christian cherub or a Celtic elf. But this is His island, and here He rules. He welcomed our ancestors three hundred years ago."

David picked up his wineglass and studied it. "Interesting. I noticed these are very old. Like your plates and silverware."

"Old, *wi*," said Joseph. "But common utensils in their day. Not all ships carried treasure, and their captains did not eat from golden plates. But Cayes Squellette's wealth is her children. And Esu is God as a child."

"Why do you call it Skeleton Cay?" asked Robert.

"That will no doubt become clear to you after Laurent's ceremony."

"Interesting," said David. "The child-god concept, I mean. The Christian religion is one of the few that doesn't offer God in a child's incarnation. Basically, you have 'Christ is born in Bethlehem,' then He disappears from the Bible until He's a man."

"Perhaps he was apprenticed to Joseph as a carpenter?" suggested Angélique.

David chucked. "Hardly an impressive résumé for the Son of God. No wonder they kept it a secret."

"Lord Krishna herded cows in his youth," said Joseph. "And there are many stories of Buddha as a boy, playing and having adventures."

"God as a child must be cherished," said Jeanette. "Protected and cared for as well as worshiped." She smiled and patted Tomas's bottom. "He needs love and affection. A culture that does not treat its children as gods is sowing the seeds of its own destruction."

"But what can a child do for you?" asked David.

Jeanette raised an eyebrow. "Do you not have a child of your own?"

Then the white men sat up in surprise as the evening quiet was broken by a sudden mechanical roar. "It is only our truck." Joseph laughed. "Not a demon from hell."

Tomas jumped down from his box, but Angélique caught him before he could run. "*Non*, little imp, it is past your bedtime."

"Dammit!" yelled Tomas. "I never have any fun around here!"

"Hush. You will have a whole night of fun at Laurent's ceremony."

Joseph laughed again. "God as a child also needs guidance occasionally."

David peered through the doorway as the truck clattered past in the starlight outside. "Er . . . my son seems to be going somewhere with yours. And that muscular boy, Pogo."

"So I see," said Joseph. "Your son has the gift of making friends quickly."

David sat back in his chair. "I guess he gets lonely sometimes. His mother and I divorced years ago. She didn't like to travel. Randy lives with me on the boat. He has a computer and video games. CDs. Magazines. We don't get in each other's way."

"And what are you seeking all over the world?" asked Jeanette.

"I write books about religions."

"Ah, yes. That is what you said."

"Pardon me." David got up and went out on the porch, but the lightless truck had vanished, and its racket was fading away in the forest. He returned with Randy's shirt and shoes and a curious look on his face.

"I know where they have gone," said Jeanette. "Do not worry, *Monsieur* Benson; there is no safer place on earth. But they will probably not return until morning."

David fingered the sweaty T-shirt. "My son can be a bit wild sometimes."

"Our children are not too easily frightened," said Joseph.

"Well, I'm sure he's in good company. Thank you for the wonderful dinner, and for your patience in answering my questions. I have many more."

"Of course," said Jeanette. "Please come to see me tomorrow. And I will have Tomas show you the *ounphor* of Esu, which he keeps. Do you swim?"

"Er . . . yes." David gave Tomas a glance. "Uh, pardon another question, but do you . . . fatten . . . a child to resemble Esu?"

Joseph hoisted Tomas to his knee. "Esu chooses the keeper

of His shrine, who may be either a boy or a girl; and they hear His call around six years of age. Some have served Him until nine or ten." He rubbed Tomas's tummy. "Esu loves to share."

"Interesting. I assume your older son served him too?"

"A logical assumption, but actually it was Pogo who kept Esu's shrine before Tomas." Joseph chuckled. "Looking like God is not a requirement. Laurent is good at poetry and thinking. Perhaps your son is a thinker as well?"

David shrugged. "We don't talk much."

The rosy light of early dawn filtered through the silvery waterfall, brightening the grotto to emerald green. Four boys lay naked and glistening with spray upon the soft carpet of moss. Three of them slept in a tangle, while the fourth was awake and seemed to watch over His slumbering friends. Randy awoke and sat up. His blue eyes roamed for a moment, then met and returned Esu's gaze. He smiled as if sharing a secret, then gently shook Pogo. "Are you awake, *mwen frè?*"

Pogo stretched like a sleepy cheetah. "I am now." He sat up and seemed to remember something. "What was it Esu said to you that was so funny?"

"But you were there. Outside in the pool with us."

"I only heard you laughing together."

Randy opened his mouth to speak, but then paused and

looked puzzled. "Swear to god, man, I knew *everything* a second ago, but I can't remember anything now."

Pogo laughed. "What is your name?"

"Huh? . . . Oh." Randy laughed too. "I mean all that *other* stuff."

"I know what you mean. But I do not think you would be happy in life if you did remember all of it. That would be more of a curse than a blessing." He nudged Laurent, who yawned.

"Um," said Randy, "that *was* a dream, wasn't it? Playin' out there in the stars an' all? Like a Navajo peyote ceremony? Except with your magic beer."

Laurent slowly stretched. "I have no idea what Navajos do. But can three people share the same dream?"

Pogo poked Randy's soft roll of stomach. "And there is the only thing magic about our beer."

"Well," said Randy, "did you hear what Esu told me, Laurent?"

"Some kind of joke, the way you where laughing."

"Will your father be worried?" asked Pogo.

Randy gazed out through the falling water. "Naw. One time I smoked crack in Miami and wandered around for a week stayin' high. He thought I was down in my cabin."

Pogo shook his head. "Some of the *ri-timoun*, the homeless street children in Port-au-Prince, sniff glue when they are lonely."

"Funny," said Randy, looking around at the empty bottles. "I don't feel hungover or nothin'." He stretched. "Fact is, I feel really good."

Pogo smiled. "Playing with Esu is like that."

Laurent got to his feet. "Pogo will make us breakfast."

The boys said good-bye to Esu, slipped into the water, dove under the fall, and swam across the pool. Randy and Pogo boosted Laurent up onto the truck. Then Pogo went around to crank.

"Can I help?" asked Randy. "That looks hard."

Pogo grinned and puffed his chest. "I am harder!" He took hold of the handle and braced his feet. "Wake up, beast!" The engine fired like a shotgun blast, blowing red flame and black smoke from its pipe. The crank spun backward, hurling Pogo into the ferns at the edge of the pool.

"*Bastaèd!*" he yelled. "*Enbesil!* Dammit to hell!"

Randy pushed through the ferns with Laurent close behind. "Pogo! Are you okay?"

Pogo struggled to sit up. "I . . . *Shit!*"

Randy grabbed his shoulders. "Pogo!"

"*Ow!* My arm is broken!"

Laurent knelt beside him. "We'll take you to Jeanette. . . . Um, maybe it's not really broken?"

"Oh yes," said Pogo ruefully. "It is very goddamn broken."

• • •

It was evening and three days later. Everyone on Cayes Squellette was gathered on the beach. The big motor yacht had been moved toward the cliffs, and the battered old schooner now rode at anchor out near the mouth of the cove. The people had formed two rows in the sand, and David Benson and Robert MacRae stood with Jeanette at the water-line. David had a cassette recorder, and Robert a small movie camera. David turned to Jeanette after glancing at Pogo, who was standing nearby with his arm in a sling.

"Is Randy the only one who can do this?" asked David.

It was clearly a question he'd asked before, but Jeanette only smiled. "The part is performed by the next in line to have the ceremony. And your son is the same age as Pogo." She looked at Iris, who was at Pogo's side. "My daughter's rite will follow Pogo's, so she will play the part for his. Perhaps she could play it now for Laurent; but no child has ever performed it twice, and it seems unfair to ask."

"I could still do it," said Pogo. "I have been teaching Randy, and my other arm is perfectly cool."

"Do not be an ass," said Iris. "You would only hurt your-self again."

"I didn't know you cared."

"You do not know a lot, stupid boy."

"What about him?" asked David, pointing to André. "He's much stronger than Randy."

"He has had his ceremony," said Jeanette. "He knows the pain, and would not want to hurt another again."

"But who did it to him?"

"Laurent did it for him."

David shook his head. "I don't understand. It's backward. In America it would be the other way around."

Jeanette smiled again. "That would be revenge. And 'vengeance is *mine*, sayeth the Lord.' . . . Of course you are free to change your mind."

"It was Randy's decision."

"Ah, *wi*," said Jeanette. "You do not get in each other's way."

Robert was checking his camera but paused to give David a one-sided smile. "This isn't going to be seen as 'politically correct' in the good ol' U.S.A., you know?"

"But it is the truth," said Jeanette. "And Esu seems to have chosen your son to remind us of that."

David raised an eyebrow. "Are you saying that He brought us here for this?"

Jeanette only shrugged. "You are here now." She looked to the cove, where the longboat was tied against the schooner. Two boys came out on the schooner's deck, and all the people went silent.

"It begins," said Jeanette.

The boys were Laurent and Randy, but it seemed as if

their friendship of the last few days had savagely ended. Laurent was naked; and the black iron manacles clamped on his wrists, and the two feet of chain connecting them, were so huge and medieval-looking that they might have been made of papier-mâché, if they hadn't been so obviously heavy. Randy wore only his jeans and, despite his softness, looked fierce and cruel with a whip in his hand. He seemed to pause as if taking a breath, and then he swung the whip with all his strength; and the crack of leather against Laurent's back came echoing over the water. David winced, but Robert was already filming; and all the people were watching in silence. David switched on his tape as Jeanette waded into the transparent wavelets and began to speak. She had told this story many times, yet her voice was clear and filled with emotion, and her words were starkly punctuated by the crack of the whip and Randy's curses as Laurent climbed clumsily into the boat, burdened by his massive shackles, and took up the heavy oars.

"Long ago there was a slave ship. She had come from Africa, bringing our people in chains to be sold like animals by those who called themselves civilized Christians. Upon reaching these waters, the ship was beset by a savage storm. She was beaten by mountainous waves, whipped by a howling wind, and slashed by rain that cut like knives. She was dismasted. Most of her crew were lost. She was sinking, and yet our people were imprisoned below in the flooding holds. They were chained to the planking. They could not escape. Many—men, women, children, babies—were drowned as the water rose."

Pogo gazed out on the water. He'd attended these rites since babyhood; but he could still almost hear the crash of the sea, the roar of the wind, the desperate screams and cries of the people below and the sounds of their chains in the darkness. Maybe Randy's father could hear it—he seemed transfixed while he held his recorder. And even Robert's face looked grim as he aimed the camera's indifferent eye. Pogo felt Iris's hand on his arm.

Jeanette continued: "Only the captain and one of his crewmen remained alive on deck, clinging to the stumps of the masts, while the wreckage of spars entangled in rigging pounded the hull and gashed at the planks. Without sail, the ship was helpless, a drifting hulk at the mercy of the elements."

Jeanette turned to point; and Pogo looked beyond the cove, as did all the other people. He could almost see the stormy sky superimposed on the gold of sunset, the raging waves seething over the rocks, and the dismasted ship with its human cargo being driven relentlessly toward them.

"The ship was cast upon the reef. She began to break up. Not many were left alive in the holds. Men fought to keep their heads above water, to help their women and children breathe. They tried to tear loose their chains from the ring bolts. The women held babies over their heads as long as they could, but most of the children had already drowned. On deck above, the last crewman was swept overside. A longboat was still lashed aboard, but the captain could not launch it alone, nor row it ashore by himself."

Jeanette paused, gazing out to sea, not seeming to notice the actual longboat, now halfway to the beach, or Laurent in chains struggling to row it while Randy cursed and whipped him.

"Desperate to save his own life, the captain knelt at the grating and called down into the hold: He would release the remaining men if they would agree to launch the boat and row it ashore."

Iris was gripping Pogo's hand, but Pogo's eyes were locked on the longboat. Laurent was pouring sweat. Blood was running down his back and dripping from his wrists, where the iron cuffs were chafing. Randy was drenched in sweat of his own from the effort of swinging the whip. He stood in the stern, his small chest heaving, his pale hair lank on his shoulders. The whip was dangling limp in his hand, but he lashed his captive with curses. Pogo thought of all the blood that must have soaked into the boat's ancient wood. Did it now have a soul of its own, he wondered, a spirit to give Laurent strength? He was only a boy who liked poetry, brave as a lion but not as strong. How could he ever make it to shore?

Jeanette continued: "The captain wanted men. What use were women and babies? But by then there were only three men, and three women with infants in arms, left alive. With his ship being battered to pieces, the captain had no choice. He unbarred the grating and threw down the keys." Jeanette now pointed to the boat. "The people were still in manacles, which were riveted around their wrists. Yet somehow the boat was launched."

Pogo watched the longboat, now only a hundred feet from the sand. Randy seemed too exhausted to swing the whip anymore, and Laurent's oar strokes were shallow and weak, sometimes just skimming the surface and hardly moving the boat at all.

Robert murmured to David in English: "What if he doesn't make it?"

"Interesting," said David. "It's not a driver's license test. He can't take it over again."

But Jeanette went on, as if never doubting Laurent's strength. "The captain was heavily armed, of course. His pistols were wet and useless, but he had a sword and a club and a whip. He would have cast the babies into the sea but feared that the women would not row, and so had allowed the infants to be placed in the bottom of the boat. His confidence began to return as the boat reached the cove in safety. He had lost his ship, and with it his world, but he still had slaves to serve him."

All of the village was silent as the longboat finally grounded on sand. Simone looked as if she would run to Laurent, but her mother held on to her hand. Laurent's father was trembling but stood with his arms around Angélique. The only sounds were Laurent's panting breaths intermingled with Randy's, the lapping of waves on the shore, and the rush of the waterfall back in the forest. Children clung to their parents. Older boys and girls held hands. The tape recorder and camera went on with their civilized sounds. Randy cursed Laurent again, bawling commands in a hoarse, breaking voice.

Jeanette continued: "The captain began to make plans. He would take this island for his own, as if all the world was his by right and his god approved of stealing. But even though our people were chained, he knew he must never show weakness before them. They must always know who was master."

Pogo watched as Laurent struggled over the side of the boat and staggered to shore. The heavy links of his manacles tangled between his legs. Maybe there were tears on his cheeks, but the sweat camouflaged them. Just as six men and women had done, he lay face-down in the shallow water while Randy walked over his back, grinding sand into his gashes. His chubby fists clenched in agony, but he made no sound.

Jeanette's quiet voice cut the silence. "Then Esu appeared."

The people had already turned around, but it took a moment for David and Robert to tear their eyes from the scene at the shoreline. Robert recovered first and swung the camera toward the trees. He seemed to have trouble keeping it steady as Esu came out of the shadowy forest and stalked between the rows of people. There seemed to be something wrong with that image, as if such a boy should be happy and skipping. But He walked with a grim sense of purpose, a frightening thing for a child to do. David's hand shook as he held the recorder. Tomas had shown them the *ounphor*, of course, and Robert had taken pictures, but they obviously hadn't expected to see Esu Himself out here on the beach—an ebony eight-year-old boy with horns, and a face full of god-like wrath.

Laurent still lay in the lapping water, which was now tinted pink by his blood. He had struggled up onto his elbows to gaze at Esu in awe. Randy's face was frozen in fear, as if he'd forgotten who he was and was no longer playing a role. The whip slipped out of his fingers; and he seemed to want to run away, but there was nowhere to go. David tensed as Esu reached out and touched Randy's chest with a fingertip.

"You have no heart," said Esu. His voice was quiet but seemed to echo—and why would God need to shout? "Die the death you deserve."

Randy dropped like a stone, as if his heart had been instantly stopped. It didn't look like acting: He fell face-down and lay deathly still. David stiffened in shock; but Jeanette only said, "Until you become as little children, you shall not enter into the kingdom of heaven." Then she knelt at Esu's feet, as did all the other islanders. Only David and Robert stood, as if uncertain of what to do.

Jeanette spread her arms to the sky. "Esu welcomed our ancestors, three men, three women, and a trio of babies. And here we have lived in peace ever since."

Esu stepped to Laurent over Randy's body. Laurent rose to his knees, and the manacles slipped from his bloody wrists to fall open in the sand. The people began to shout and cheer as they gathered around the three small figures. David seemed to catch his breath and started toward his son, but Laurent and Pogo reached him first. They lifted his face from the sand. Then Esu touched his chest again. Randy's eyes fluttered open. "Did I do well?" he asked in Kreyol.

Esu giggled. "You were very cool."

"Thank you, my brother," said Laurent. "Now I am a

man." He kissed Randy's cheek, then gave Esu a hug and thanked Him too.

"You may do the dishes next week," said Esu.

David switched off his recorder and wiped the sweat from his face. "Is it over?" he asked Jeanette.

"Except for the feast, which will last until morning. There will be drums and dancing." Esu came to Jeanette, who hugged him and added, "The children are now in charge. We must serve them and do what they say."

"I've seen a lot of feasts," said David. "I have to get back to the boat and make notes."

"Surely you do not fear children?"

"That's not what I meant."

Robert had picked up the ancient slave chains. "These things were actually riveted on," he said to David in English. "How did they fall off on cue?"

David shrugged. "Any circus clown can do that trick." He seemed more interested in Esu. "That's Tomas, isn't it?" he asked Jeanette.

"He is whoever you believe him to be."

"May I touch him?"

"He would probably prefer a hug." Jeanette glanced at Randy, who along with Laurent was getting lots from everyone, boys and girls alike. "Children often do."

"I meant the horns," said David. "They're from a baby goat, aren't they?"

"Few things in nature are as joyful and naughty as kids."

Esu giggled and leaned forward to let David tug at His horns. They seemed very firmly attached. Robert came over to look. "Some sort of superglue. Painful as hell to remove."

Jeanette laughed. "Any circus clown can do that trick."

David glanced toward the distant reef. "I assume the island's name must have come from the bones washing up on the beach?"

"For years afterward," said Jeanette. "It must have been very sad for the people."

David studied Esu again. "Have you ever thought that there might be a logical explanation for him?" He waved around. "For this whole . . ."

"'Legend'?" suggested Jeanette. "Fairy tale, perhaps? A missionary once proposed that a boy had been marooned on this island. A slave child lost, or perhaps thrown overboard, from another ship years before. And this young savage killed the captain. A sneak attack, no doubt." Jeanette smiled. "And I in turn suggested that Jesus Christ might have been only the son of a carpenter with a natural talent for public speaking."

Laurent and Pogo had helped Randy up, and he stood with an arm around each of them, careful of Laurent's bleeding back. "How are you gonna have any fun at your feast?"

"Jeanette has some magical salve. And of course we have our magical beer."

David turned to his son. "Are you all right, Randy?"

"Yeah." Randy looked at Laurent and then to Pogo. "My birthday's in two months. I want to stay and have it here. I want to have my own ceremony. I'm tired of travelin' all around lookin' for God with you."

David scowled. "I'm not 'looking for God,' Randy. I just write books."

"Yeah, you are. An' what's sad is, you don't even know it."

David flushed beneath his tan and almost scowled again, but hesitated when Esu frowned. "We can talk about it. Tomorrow. Aboard the boat. I assume you want to stay for the party?"

Esu was looking at David, and the knowing expression on His face seemed far too aware for an eight-year-old. He smiled a very impish smile. "He will stay much longer than that."

WHAT IS THE DICKENS?

The air around Daddy Jack Karam's bed smelled sour as socks. But he got mad if anybody lit an incense stick or squirted lavender air freshener. "Pollute my domain!" he'd roar.

Leslie sat quietly with a book in the upholstered rocking chair by the window waiting till he woke up, because she had promised she would read out loud to him after school today. They were halfway through *Arabian Jazz*. But she was reading *The Sufi Message of Hazrat Inayat Khan* to herself. Volume 1 contained sections on "The Way of Illumination," "The Inner Life," "The Soul, Whence and Wither?" and "The Purpose of Life."

Daddy Jack had taken a glance at the table of contents a few weeks ago and remarked, "Pretty big bites! Think you can understand all that?" If she left him a note now and took off, he'd be mad. "You were in a rush, huh? You had better people to go see?"

He had never been so grumpy before his illness. He used to be the one holding a wineglass over his head at birthday parties, swiveling his hips, singing little songs. He told jokes and funny stories from his childhood in Lebanon. He complimented Leslie's friends till they felt smart and glamorous, and he rarely complained. But his illness disappointed him.

Hadn't he been a good enough guy, honest and trustworthy? Hadn't he said his prayers? When his cousin Muna brought him that book about bad things happening to good people, he hurled it to the floor. "Obviously not good enough," he said.

His bedside table: bottle of Tums, glass of half-drunk water, Walkman radio, Arabic music tapes, medicine bottles, thermometer, crumpled Kleenex. None of the artists painted this kind of still life. Should Leslie bring him grapes, figs dripping dew, a split, ripe cantaloupe? These days he said he hated food. He was drinking that awful diet stuff from small brown cans in various nasty flavors, calling it his "lifeblood." "Hand me my lifeblood, would you, honey?"

Even his favorite spiced lentil soup, made by Leslie's mom, sat for days in a plastic tub in the refrigerator. Leslie offered to mix him smoothies, fresh bananas, berries, doses of protein powder, far more delicious than canned drinks, but he wrinkled his nose. "I'm not in a fruity mood, baby, know what I mean?" He fell asleep even in the middle of conversations.

So she brought books and homework and magazines when she came to see him. Just in case. She sat with him in his room. His sinking ship. The nurse left at four o'clock, and he was alone till the next morning. The way he wanted it. Leslie's mother could not get Daddy Jack to move into their own house though they lived only a mile away.

"I *wish* Mama Jean had lived longer than Daddy Jack, don't you, Mom?" Leslie had said more than once. It felt so much easier when her grandmother was still around to take care of everything.

Nancy, Leslie's mother, sighed. Lately her sighs seemed longer and longer.

Mama Jean had died suddenly of a stroke a few years ago. One day she was rolling stuffed grape leaves for Sunday dinner and the next day—poof! Daddy Jack sat in their bedroom in the dark for weeks, refusing to talk to people or to eat much then either. But his own slow, painful departure seemed almost harder for everyone to bear.

When Leslie was five, her father had disappeared, vanished into thin air, dematerialized. Ten years ago, so Leslie was used to it by now. She never cried about him anymore, though her mother told her she had cried often, especially at bedtime, for a year. Nancy had cried too. They cried together. But Leslie no longer expected to see him coming around a twinkling corner at Christmas, his arms laden with red packages. Or pointing a hose at the blooming zinnias in their front yard when it was summer. Later her mother had told her this was the only chore he would ever do.

Leslie used to jingle his silver key ring and hide it in his tennis shoe. He would swing her high over his head to make her squeal. He wore checkered shirts and a baseball cap. Her packet of memories felt so small! She could not recall any extended conversations with her dad, though she would have preferred words to the scattered images.

Did he say, "Nobody ever had a prettier daughter," or "I will love you forever, even after I vanish like steam"? Did he tell her never to be afraid of strangers because strangers would, after all, be everywhere she went? She would live a long life among strangers. They would point out directions for her. They would sit next to her in social studies. They would be walking down the street outside Daddy Jack's sad window, clicking an umbrella's pointy tip onto the pavement, humming.

What did he ever tell her?

Daddy Jack cracked open one eyelid. "Hey babe, I got a present for you. Did you know that?"

He pulled a small blue velvet box from under his pillow.

"A ring?" Only a ring could live in a box that small.

"Mebbe, mebbe not. But you gotta do something for me first. You gotta tell me who you believe in. You gotta promise your old Daddy Jack before he checks out that you know who's God, who's Jesus, can you tell me that? Can you tell me where you put your faith?"

Put. Faith. Upper left-hand drawer? He began coughing, rumbling hideously as if his body were a rock quarry and someone had lit sticks of dynamite deep inside him.

Leslie wished she could cover her ears.

Instead, she lifted the water glass toward him.

"I believe," she said, "in water."

At home she told her mother, "He tried to bribe me. This is pathetic. Did Jesus ever say we should bribe other people to get them to say or do what we want? I feel sorry for Jesus, people saying and doing strange things in His name all the time."

Nancy, who had had her hair lightened at lunchtime to cover the encroaching gray, was staring into a mirror suffering serious pangs of regret. She said, "Right. But wouldn't you like to make Daddy Jack feel better in his last days? He doesn't have long, you know. Could be tomorrow. If you say what you know he wants to hear, he'll settle down. Go out peacefully. I mean, why not? You don't *dis*believe in Jesus, do you?"

"I believe in Jesus, but I don't believe in *his* Jesus. I don't believe in exclusionary Jesus."

Nancy sighed. "Such words . . . I look like a cheerleader, don't I?" She turned her head slowly from side to side. "Oh well, I always wanted to be one."

Leslie's father, Nancy's husband, had disappeared from a truck stop outside Uvalde, Texas. He was on a business trip, expected at a regional bank meeting in town, but he never got there.

His car was found with the keys in the ignition. The same keys Leslie used to play with. Dangling. The lady who worked the cash register inside that place said she thought he had bought a gigantic iced tea, one of those huge plastic cups that won't fit in the car's cup holder. The detectives showed the lady photographs of him, but she hadn't noticed if he'd used the rest room before or after, or if he'd talked to anyone. Cars and trucks stopped all day long; people bought gas, oil, chips. Cowboys wearing earrings used the rest room day and night. What a weird world it was now. Cowboys wearing earrings; who could ever have imagined it? The detectives grilled the clerk thoroughly, and she said, "Look, do you know how many iced teas I sell in a single day? I can't stare into the heart and soul of every customer."

Leslie's dad was not the first person to disappear from that same road. A music teacher had disappeared the year before, en route to a music educators' meeting in Alpine. His car, stuffed with boxes of sheet music, had been found alongside Highway 90 outside Del Rio. Also, an entire family had vanished a few months later—the newspaper said they might have abandoned their car to suggest foul play and hoofed it into Mexico to escape paying back taxes. Recently, in a highly publicized search, authorities had been digging up an entire ranch, looking for the remains of Madalyn Murray O'Hair, the famous atheist, and her son and granddaughter, who had been missing for years.

Sometimes Leslie read stories about the vast numbers of political disappearances of people in South American countries and thought, "I know how their families feel," though no one had ever suggested her father's case had any political overtones. Nor had they thought he was robbing the bank he worked for—not a cent came up missing.

After three years of total silence from Leslie's father, no clue or shred of evidence pointing in any direction—according to countless phone calls with some very frustrated detectives—Nancy had her husband declared dead. He hadn't had life insurance, and he hadn't, thank goodness, really had any debts, but Nancy needed "emotional closure." Now she was free to marry again, though she'd barely had a date since he disappeared. What kind of luck would she have, telling her date, "Yes, I was married, but my husband evaporated"? Nancy imagined any potential boyfriend backing away immediately. But she could hardly lie.

She started listening seriously to the blues.

Deep South gospel music, and the blues.

Privately, she told Leslie she didn't really think her dad was dead. Recently a handsome man had been found on Galveston Island, living a second life with a second wife and an assumed name, having "disappeared" from his first family back north in Iowa or somewhere. He was even doing community work. Could you believe it? That someone would abandon his own little boys to be a do-gooder elsewhere? Nancy thought Leslie's father might be doing something strange like that.

"But why? What makes you think so? Had you been fighting a lot when he left?"

"No." Nancy sighed. "We never really *fought*. He just always seemed . . . bored. Bored and restless. As if one life weren't big enough for him. I used to think, he's sorry he married me. Sorry, but too polite to say so. I think he loved *you*, though! He always wanted to be with you the minute he got home. He loved playing with you. He even combed your hair and made that funny ponytail you used to have. Not all fathers do that with girls. That's why I couldn't really understand how . . . I mean, if he left on purpose. . . . Well, he *did* hate his job, but he also appeared to have few other interests. He seemed to resent that I enjoyed my own job at the library so much. Isn't that odd? Why would anyone resent someone else liking their job? He'd look around these rooms in the evenings as if he were trapped in a cage, then pitch the newspaper onto the couch and wander outside for a while. Do the hose thing."

"Pathetic. Why would you marry such a dull guy?" Leslie liked their rooms. Their rooms had old wooden tables, little lamps, heaps of books and soft, cushiony chairs.

Oddly, Leslie had lost all sympathy for her father by now, though occasionally she wondered about him. She felt almost glad he had disappeared. What if she had had to grow up with such a boring person hovering around her? In some way disappearance seemed cleaner than divorce. Many of her friends bounced back and forth between their parents on weekends, preferring the bedroom at one house to the bedroom at the other, getting irritated when their parents dated new people.

Daddy Jack, of course, hated her father with all his might. He thought the disappearance had been intentional and blamed his son-in-law for abandoning his darling daughter and *her* darling daughter. "I never liked him from the beginning," he said, after Leslie's dad was declared dead. "I used to tell Nancy, find some nice Lebanese guy, let me spread the word through the church, one of those ladies is bound to have a nice nephew living like a king somewhere . . . give me a minute, I find you a guy. But she says no, she's stuck like glue to this bozo she met in college, for whatever reason I never know."

"But what if he *is* dead?" Leslie asked once. "What if he *did* get kidnaped, and you're saying mean things about someone who became a victim?"

Daddy Jack shook his head. He couldn't believe in that possibility. He said he had never trusted the guy—something in his eyes. Leslie thought this anger and hate had been what made him get sick with cancer, just as she thought Mama Jean's stroke had been the fault of her suppressed sorrow. Everybody held things in.

But when Daddy Jack got onto religion, you wished he'd hold things in a little more.

Leslie wrote a paper called "Religion Should Be Private" for her English class.

Obviously, her teacher wrote across the top of the paper, *you have very strong feelings about this subject. Good job!*

She read it to Daddy Jack, who said, "Naw naw naw! Religion is community, baby! We gather together in His name, blah blah blah. Why didn't your mama raise you right? I raised *her* right!"

Which was part of the problem. Nancy had been raised so well, the Maronite service every Sunday, the Sunday school, the Bible school, the fund-raisers right and left, that she was all worn out with religion by the time she had her own daughter. She called it "social religion." She usually took Leslie to church on holidays, but she didn't pay her regular membership dues, she refused to bake a cake for the bake sale, she said the old ladies and their inquisitive manners got on her nerves. She could imagine them chattering away across town. *Poor poor poor Nancy, her husband VANISHED! How can she stand it? Did he have another FAMILY? Was he a BIGAMIST?*

But when they looked in her eyes and held both her hands tightly after the Easter service, all they said was "How are you *doing*, dear? Can we help in any way?"

The little blue velvet box disappeared. Leslie didn't see it again. She asked her mother, "Was Mama Jean buried with her wedding ring on?"

Nancy said, "I think so. Why?"

Mama Jean had been a Muslim till she married Daddy Jack. She converted because he urged her to. Privately she told Nancy she had just "added something on," but never "given anything up." She still prayed five times a day to Allah in her heart. "What difference does it make what you call yourself?" she said. "Just be nice. That's my religion."

Daddy Jack kept prodding Leslie for answers. He nagged her between coughs in a garbled, gravelly voice. "You believe in heaven, don't you, baby? God, I do. It's my next stop, I hope. How you think you gonna get in there if you won't be polite to the gatekeeper? What's your big resistance? I'll miss you if you don't show up."

Often when he talked like this, Leslie didn't answer. Or sometimes she said things like "I am not resisting. I am just not . . . sure."

One day she laid two fat jalapeño peppers from Daddy Jack's pepper bush on his white bedspread, right in his lap. All these extra peppers this year—they were beautiful to look at, even if you didn't eat them all. Another day she arranged a vase of hopeful tuberoses on the table by the window. They had such a strong hypnotic odor, particularly at sundown—maybe they would help his room.

Mystery did not bother her. She said this out loud. "I like mysteries. It's my birthright! Mystery father. Mystery books, mystery movies, mystery religion. Why do people have to act so sure about things? How can they act so sure? I think they're pretending!" Mystery was more comforting to her than conviction.

Daddy Jack howled like a wolf. He said, "Chinese check-ers, baby. Bring the board over here. Play me a game. Take me out of my mystery—my misery—whatever."

On Friday a priest stood visiting at Daddy Jack's bedside when Leslie arrived. Did this mean the end was near?

"Here she is." Daddy Jack introduced them, though Leslie had seen this priest at the Maronite church more than once. The priest tipped his serious gaze to her and held her hand too tightly, the way people do to convince you they have a backbone. His fleshy palm felt sweaty and hot.

She thought words that made her feel guilty: Heaven's Paw. Piggo Priest. What had Daddy Jack said about her before she got there? And when was her mother getting off work from the library? *Help!* Nancy always stopped in on her way home. Often their visits crisscrossed, and they rode home together. Some Fridays Nancy got off early, and she and Leslie went straight out to an early bird dinner together after they'd been to Daddy Jack's.

"Leslie, please sit down," the priest said. He motioned her to the upholstered chair by the window, as if she'd never seen it before.

"Yes, I know, I sit here all the time."

"Your grandfather has told me you might have some

questions about our savior. Feel free, Leslie; you know that's what I'm here for."

She opened her eyes wide. Was it? Had he been invited over simply because Daddy Jack knew she was coming by? Or was he giving the last rites, and Leslie was just a footnote?

Gigantic gray doves tipped the bird feeder from side to side beyond Daddy Jack's big window. They flapped and fluttered, trying to get some seed by sitting on the feeder's roof and poking their beaks down. They were too large to sit on the little ledge.

"I *hate* how people fight in the name of religion and then want to be respected for their holiness," she blurted out, surprising herself. Had she even been thinking about this lately? Not much. But her words tumbled forward magically. "Like in Lebanon, Christians and Muslims fighting for so many years, and the fundamentalists fighting everywhere and the Jews arguing in Jerusalem, all those orthodox guys hating the Arabs most and thinking they're holy in their black coats, and forever down through history if you look at history and especially I hate it when people think their religion has to be the best religion and so far I haven't found many people who don't, except the Sufis, whom I love a lot because 'The Sufi tolerates all' and does not claim his own religion as the best and the Bahais and the Unitarians feel this way too but we don't go to the

Unitarian Church much because it's too far on the edge of town and I'm not even very impressed by the milk bottles lately."

"The *what*?"

"You know the Holy Acres Dairy Farm over at Devine that sells milk in those old-fashioned very nice milk bottles that you have to leave a dollar deposit on and they have all the flavors like peach milk and Aztec milk, which is coffee-flavored, and strawberry milk and chocolate. . . ."

Daddy Jack was staring at her as if she'd lost her mind.

"Well." She gulped. "They put Bible verses on their bottles. That's okay. I mean, they're free to do that if they want to. But then I heard that the man who owns the dairy gives a lot of money to fundamentalist causes, people trying to manipulate what is and isn't taught in our schools, for example, and I told Mom we can't buy that milk anymore. Too bad, because it's the best milk."

The priest said, "Leslie, you must respect that man's faith. It sounds to me as if you are holding his faith against him."

"I respect faiths. But I don't respect fundamentalists. They're too certain about everything! Certainty is fake! And I certainly don't respect secret undercover manipulation. I don't respect people who try to get other people to do what they want in the so-called spirit of religion even if it's little stuff and especially if they think they're smarter which is what they always think." She found herself glaring at her dying grandfather. He was thin as spaghetti. Maybe she *was* losing her mind.

The priest was nice enough to keep listening to her, though he looked confused.

She pulled her book from her Mexican satchel. "Listen to this! From Hazrat Inayat Khan."

"Who?"

Daddy Jack snorted, "She likes him because his name's exotic!"

"The Sufi mystic. You know, mystical Islam. From our old part of the world. The Middle East. You know?"

Both men stared at her without speaking.

Leslie held the book pages open toward them, "I read this all the time. See how marked up it is? Great stuff." Then she read aloud, "'The true lover of God keeps his love silently hidden in his heart, like a seed sown in the ground; and if the seedling grows, it grows in his actions toward his fellow man. He cannot act except with kindness, he cannot feel anything but forgiveness; every movement he makes, everything he does, speaks of his love, but not his lips.'"

She slapped the yellow book shut.

"I mean, look at it this way—God knows all things, right? Don't you say that? So where is my dad? If God knows, why wouldn't He or She tell us? It's a mystery! Lips shut tight! It's been a mystery for ten years! So I prefer to let God and all His or Her Messengers stay mysterious too. Because that's how they feel to me. I pray to . . . trees."

"Merciful heavens!" Daddy Jack exploded, coughing hard behind his hand. "Sam, I told you, talk some sense into her! We're losing our hold!"

"Transcendentalism." The priest shook his head, sweating harder now. He pulled his collar away from his neck, sniffing. "What *is* that fragrant smell in here? These flowers? Is there a fan? Could we put your air-conditioning on? It's hot as the dickens."

Father Sam and Daddy Jack. Their names sounded like party treats or fish plates at Sea Island Restaurant. Leslie burst out laughing. "What," she asked, "is the dickens?"

Later Nancy would say that she came into the house and saw a shimmery woman sitting on the couch wearing Mama Jean's favorite old dress, but it was not Mama Jean. She was not saying it was an angel or a bona fide apparition. Maybe it was just a reflection, a mirage. Maybe the curtains created an optical illusion that looked like a dress.

The vision, the sudden sweet heat, or something else, caused Nancy to pass out onto the floor. She had never fainted before, not even when her husband vanished. Leslie heard the thud, ran to the front room, and screamed. Nancy had hit the coffee table with her forehead. A bloody cut marked her forehead over the right eyebrow.

Father Sam dialed 911 as Leslie ran for a cold towel. She threw the whole thing over her mother's head and flopped to the floor beside her, feeling for a pulse, which was definitely still there, pounding away. Leslie squeezed her mother's hand and shook her arm.

"Mama, Mama, wake up, please!"

Are these endless unexpected moments tucked securely under the edge of every scene, just waiting for a chance to slide into view?

Nancy finally opened her eyes with difficulty, squinting. "Where am I?" By the time the ambulance came wailing to the door—was it four minutes? five?—Daddy Jack had died.

So the person they came for was not the person they ended up working on. Such a mysterious household the medical attendants entered! Even the priest seemed slightly ill. They doctored Nancy's cut and took her vitals, and listened as she groggily insisted there was another person present as well.

But she wasn't sure who the woman was. And they couldn't find her.

Then they had to tend to Daddy Jack. The priest kept saying, "We were just having a conversation! I stepped out of the room only for a moment. . . ."

Later, days later, after more mysteries than anyone would ever be able to count had happened in the world, after Daddy Jack's funeral, at which Leslie read a passage from Khalil Gibran, just as her grandfather had asked her to, and Nancy read a poem by Nizar Qabbani from Syria, who had died only recently himself, a small blue box was found on Daddy Jack's bedside table.

Leslie could have sworn it was not sitting there when she had her last visit with him and the priest. She kept trying to remember what her last words had been before Nancy entered the house, since those were the last words she spoke to Daddy Jack, but she could not recall.

She almost thought she shouldn't open the box.

"Go ahead," her mother said.

Inside was an ancient gold coin, inscribed with Arabic lettering, with a small note folded underneath.

The note, in a contorted, tiny script, said, "Leslie, I'll pray for you. From wherever I am. Okay? I love you. Daddy Jack. P.S. You can always change your mind. This is yours anyway."

Any Way. All the ways. The avenues, alleyways, paths, bypasses, and beaten trails. The crumpled maps and lost routes.

Where did people spend gold coins these days if they weren't pirates?

A deep quietude settled over the room. They were packing Jack's clothes in boxes to take to the homeless shelter.

Nancy lifted the coin from Leslie and turned it over in her hands. "Where in the world? He must have had this in his sock drawer or his safety deposit box for years. It's heavy! Feel how heavy it is!"

"Yes," said Leslie, holding it, the thick ancient heft of it, up to her cheek. The feeling of missing him blew over her like a strong wind for the first intense time since he had died. She closed her eyes.

She would never again hear his voice on this earth. *Honey. Baby.* The rueful laugh. Now all her daddies were gone. Into the mystery forever far and near. She would carry him inside her ear, where he would grow fainter and fainter, as she stood under the billowing leaves of summer, as she drank cool water from her own tall glass.

About the authors

NANCY SPRINGER is the author of numerous novels and stories, including fantasy, mystery (for which she has received two Edgar Allan Poe awards), magical realism, and mainstream work. In whatever genre, much of her fiction deals with questions of religion and spirituality, although as a teenager she would have sworn on a stack of Bibles that she was an atheist. Since then she has been married to (and later divorced from) a Lutheran minister, occasioning a few "brushes with religion" in her own life. The idea for "The Boy Who Called God She" emerged during an argument with a fundamentalist Christian concerning the nature of a living deity.

Nancy's latest novel for adults is *Plumage*, about a middle-aged woman going through adolescence. Her latest novel for young adults is *Sky Rider*, about an angel on horseback. Working on a series about the daughter of Robin Hood, Springer lives in Dallastown, Pennsylvania, with five freethinking felines.

· · ·

Born in Albany, New York, where he attended Catholic schools for thirteen years and then directed music for church services at his local parish, **GREGORY MAGUIRE** now lives in Concord, Massachusetts, with his partner and their son. Maguire is the author of two novels for adults: *Wicked: The Life and Times of the Wicked Witch of the West* and *Confessions of an Ugly Stepsister*, and a dozen books for children, including *The Good Liar* and *Missing Sisters*. The poem quoted in "Chatterbox" is by his stepmother, Marie McAuliff Maguire, and is used with permission.

   Despite the fact that Gregory once scooped ice cream at Friendly's, no characters in the story are based on actual individuals, living or dead, except, perhaps, the ineffable presence in the church, to whom in this story no lines are ascribed.

· · ·

VIRGINIA EUWER WOLFF's novels have all been selected as ALA Best Books for Young Adults or ALA Notable Books for Young Readers, sometimes both. Among her prizes are the International Reading Association Award (for *Probably Still Nick Swansen*), the Janus Korczak Book Award Honor from the Anti-Defamation League (for *The Mozart Season*), the Golden Kite, the Bank Street Prize, the *Booklist* Top of the List (for *Make Lemonade*), and the Jane Addams Award from the

Women's International League for Peace and Freedom (for *Bat 6*). Her new book is *True Believer*, a sequel to *Make Lemonade*.

The daughter of a Presbyterian organist, Virginia has played the violin in ensembles for religious oratorios and masses at Unitarian, Presbyterian, and Episcopal services and at Jewish, Catholic, Methodist, Baptist, and nonsectarian weddings. She lives in Oregon.

• • •

When **MARILYN SINGER** was nine, she voluntarily did a report comparing several world religions. Since then she's been interested in how, what, and why people believe. The author of over fifty children's and young adult books, Marilyn's works include poetry, fantasies, mysteries, realistic fiction, nonfiction, and picture books. *I Believe in Water: Twelve Brushes with Religion* is the second anthology she has compiled and edited.

Born in the Bronx and now a resident of Brooklyn, New York, and Litchfield County, Connecticut, Marilyn has varied interests that include bird- and other animal-watching, hiking, going to the cinema and theater, playing CD-ROM adventure games, and training her standard poodle Easy for obedience shows. She is married to Steve Aronson, her best friend and critic. Marilyn is currently the host of the

America Online Children's Writers Chat. Her web address is: http://users.aol.com/writerbabe/marilyn.htm. Please visit!

• • •

JACQUELINE WOODSON is the author of a number of books for children and young adults, including *Miracle's Boys*, *If You Come Softly*, *I Hadn't Meant to Tell You This*, and *From the Notebooks of Melanin Sun*. She is the recipient of two Coretta Scott King Honors and two Jane Addams Peace Award Honors and lives in Brooklyn, New York.

About "On Earth" Jacqueline says, "I've always wanted to write about my experience growing up a Jehovah's Witness, and while 'On Earth' is not completely autobiographical, there is an element of autobiography to it. My years as a Witness were complicated ones. Years I neither regret nor miss. Being a Witness is a part of my young adult world that remains with me—tender and complex as adolescence itself."

• • •

MARGARET PETERSON HADDIX is the author of *Leaving Fishers*, which tells the story of a girl who gets involved in a cultlike religious group. Like several of her other books, *Leaving Fishers* was named an ALA Best Book for Young Adults and an *American Bookseller* Pick of the Lists. Another of her books, *Don't You Dare to Read This, Mrs. Dunphrey*, won the International Reading Association Children's Book Award.

Margaret has worked as a newspaper reporter, a newspaper copy editor, and a community college instructor. She's lived in Ohio, Indiana, Illinois, Pennsylvania, and—briefly during college—Luxembourg. She and her husband have two young children, which means that she regularly grapples with questions like "If God made us, who made God?" She also teaches Sunday school, which only compounds the questioning.

Margaret has joked that she began writing for kids instead of adults because, as she approached thirty, she finally figured out the answers to many of the problems of adolescence. But, she says, "I expect to struggle for the rest of my life with the quandaries I explored in 'Going Through the Motions.'"

• • •

KYOKO MORI is the author of two coming-of-age novels, *Shizuko's Daughter* and *One Bird* (both ALA Notable Books), as well as two nonfiction books for adults, *The Dream of Water* and *Polite Lies*. Her awards include the Best Novel of the Year from the Wisconsin Council of Writers, the Paterson Award for Young Adult Novels, and the *Hungry Mind Review* Young Adult Novel of Distinction. She lives in Cambridge, Massachusetts, and attends the Unitarian Universalist church on Sundays unless she is out bird-watching in Mt. Auburn Cemetery. She believes that beauty, quietness, and openmindedness are the most important elements in her pursuit of spiritual sustenance.

"Forty-nine Days" grew out of her fascination with the language of the Psalms, her work as a songbird rehabilitator a few years ago in Wisconsin, and her memories of summers spent with her Buddhist grandparents in Japan. After living twenty years in Japan and twenty-two years in the American Midwest, Kyoko moved to Cambridge in May 1999 to teach creative writing at Harvard University.

• • •

Award-winning author **JENNIFER ARMSTRONG** was raised in a church just like that of her character Monica. It was a Presbyterian Church, with a classic steeple and a pretty good choir. Her fondest memories of her church days were the potluck suppers, and thus her ideas about religion have little to do with doctrine but much to do with scalloped potatoes and meatloaf and being neighborly. She makes her home in Saratoga Springs, New York, with a Jewish husband and various dogs of unknown denomination. She has never yet mutilated a garden gnome, but the thought has crossed her mind. . . .

Among her books are: *Shipwreck at the Bottom of the World*, a *Boston Globe–Horn Book* Honoree for Nonfiction and winner of the Orbis Pictus Award; *Chin Yu Min and the Ginger Cat*, an ALA Notable Book; *The Dreams of Mairhe Mehan*, winner of the *Hungry Mind* Books of Distinction award; and the young readers' adaptation of Peter Jennings's best-selling *The Century—The Century for Young People*.

• • •

JOYCE CAROL THOMAS's young adult novels include the multiple-award-winning *Marked by Fire*, *Bright Shadow*, *Water Girl*, *The Golden Pasture*, *Journey*, and *When the Nightingale Sings*. She is also editor of *A Gathering of Flowers: Stories About Being Young in America*, to which she contributed the short story "Young Reverend Zelma Lee Moses."

Joyce recalls when she wrote "Handling Snakes": "While I was a professor of creative writing at the University of Tennessee in Knoxville, I was fortunate to have two dear white housekeepers. They worked at getting me giggling or sighing by telling me scandalous and scary stories from the hills and mountains of poverty-stricken white America. Once they offered to drag me down to the hollers to visit a snake-handling church. From that invitation my imagination conjured up 'Handling Snakes.'"

Her web site is http://www.joycecarolthomas.com.

• • •

M. E. KERR was born in Auburn, New York, attended Stuart Hall in Staunton, Virginia, and was graduated from the University of Missouri. She was the 1993 recipient of the

Margaret A. Edwards award for lifetime achievement, and in 1996 she was awarded an honorary Ph.D. in English Literature from Long Island University.

While she is very interested in religion, she is not religious.

Her web site is http://www.columbia.edu/~MSK28/

• • •

JESS MOWRY was born in Mississippi and raised in Oakland, California. In 1988 he bought a used typewriter and began writing stories for and about the street kids in a neighborhood shelter where he worked. Since then he has had seven books published in eight languages and many short stories published in various magazines and anthologies. He cowrote the screenplay for a produced feature-length film based upon his novel *Way Past Cool*, and has also written several other screenplays, a stage play, and a live theatrical project about street and gang kids. His seventh novel, *Bones Become Flowers*, is about homeless children in Haiti, where he helped to open a children's refuge and school.

The story "Esu's Island" reflects his belief in the good, spiritual power of Voodoo. He divides his time between writing and working with kids in Haiti and in Oakland.

• • •

NAOMI SHIHAB NYE majored in the study of world religions at Trinity University after a delightfully ecumenical childhood. Her recent books include *Fuel* (poems), *Habibi* (a novel for teens that won five Best Books awards), and *Lullaby Raft* (a picture book). She has edited six prize-winning anthologies of poetry for young readers, including *This Same Sky*; *The Tree Is Older Than You Are*; *The Space Between Our Footsteps: Poems & Paintings from the Middle East*; *What Have You Lost?*, and *Salting the Ocean*. She lives in downtown San Antonio, Texas, a block from the river, with her husband, photographer Michael Nye, and their thirteen-year-old son.

	DATE DUE		